SMOKE COVER

Other books by Dorothy P. O'Neill:

L is for Love
Double Deception
Fatal Purchase
Ultimate Doom

SMOKE COVER

•

Dorothy P. O'Neill

AVALON BOOKS
NEW YORK

PRINTED IN THE UNITED STATES OF AMERICA
ON ACID-FREE PAPER
BY HADDON CRAFTSMEN, BLOOMSBURG, PENNSYLVANIA

Thanks to Mary and Bill Barlow, Diane and Dwight Barlow, Roger Barlow, Jack O'Neill, and Patricia and Toby Taylor.

Each of you contributed something to this book—professional and technical advice, help with situations familiar to your own generation, and, most importantly, ongoing encouragement.

Prologue

Manhattan, mid-May

In the kitchen of the spacious uptown residence where the Hunterdon family had lived for three generations, Fannie watched the new cook plop her fat rump onto a chair and glance around. There was no mistaking the look of disapproval in her watery blue eyes. When she'd given everything a good once-over, she peered across the table at Fannie.

She's picked up on my dark skin and she's going to ask what country I came from, Fannie thought. She'd set this fat cook straight. "I'm American," she'd say. "Some of my people were living in this country before Christopher Columbus even heard about it, and some came here on slave ships."

Maybe the cook figured it out for herself. Instead of asking questions, she said, "At the employment bureau I was told this was a very rich home, but you'd think they didn't have a quid. This old hole looks like it hasn't been done up since Queen Victoria was on the throne."

Fannie's indignation rose. Where did this woman get off, calling the Hunterdon home a hole? Like she'd worked in Queen Victoria's castle. Maybe she was English. She talked funny.

1

"The refrigerator's new," Fannie said, defensively. "And the stove's only a couple of years old."

The new cook gave a sniff. "They're nowheres near each other, or the sink, either. I'll wear out me boots getting a meal together in this place. The last home where I worked—the Duke of Talkington's grand London house it was—the kitchen was done up all new."

Fannie brushed a lock of her graying hair away from her eyes and adjusted her bifocals for a better appraisal of the new cook. This one had her nose in the air, all right. And she'd only arrived, bag and baggage, this morning, and was hardly into her room in the servants' quarters before she started asking how many were on the staff, and what their pay was. Fannie skirted around the pay question. Her salary was none of this woman's business.

"Right now it's just me," she said. "The butler's retired and the chambermaid left to get married. We're getting replacements."

The new cook, Myrtle her name was, didn't need to know they'd both quit, or that there'd been a parade of servants in and out of the house ever since old Mrs. Hunterdon died and Miss Harriet took over. Replacements weren't easy to get, anymore. Fannie was sure the word had gotten out about Miss Harriet's rotten disposition. By now she had a bad reputation with the employment agency which two generations of Hunterdons had used for years. It was surprising they'd sent this Myrtle over. Maybe she was in a hurry for a job and they didn't have any place else to send her.

Fannie hoped it would be awhile before Miss Harriet had a row with Myrtle and she quit. They couldn't be without a cook when they were already without a chambermaid. So far, the agency hadn't sent anyone over for that. Fat, high-nosed Myrtle wouldn't like it when she found out she had to pitch in with cleaning the bedrooms and bathrooms.

Myrtle's voice came into her musings. "At the employment bureau they told me the lady's a *countess*. What's she like?"

Fannie decided to answer only the query about Miss Harriet being a countess. The nosey cook would soon find out for herself what Miss Harriet was like.

"Yes, she's the Countess Zanardi," she replied. A wry smile joined the wrinkles on her face. Miss Harriet had refused to be called Contessa. It had been nine years since she divorced her second husband, Count Paolo Zanardi, yet she still kept his name instead of going back to Hunterdon like she did after she got rid of that football player who was husband number one. Fannie suspected Miss Harriet was as happy to get rid of football player Gus Stanky's name as she was to be free of the man, himself.

Miss Harriet stayed friends with both husbands, especially Zanardi. Like a gigolo, he was, living high on the divorce settlement money and Miss Harriet calling on him whenever she needed an escort to some fancy party. But Myrtle didn't have to know about that, either, Fannie decided.

"Countess Zanardi," Myrtle murmured. Clearly, she was impressed with Miss Harriet's title. She didn't know, yet, that Miss Harriet wasn't born a countess. What would she think when she found out Miss Harriet had divorced the count but not his title?

"And that woman who interviewed me—is she a family member? Does she have a title, too?" Myrtle asked.

"That woman was Mrs. Locke. We call her Miss Jane." Fannie replied. "She doesn't have a title. She's not a family member. She's an old friend of the countess, been living here more than nine years. She's in charge of running the house."

Myrtle looked disappointed. She would have loved working in a home with two countesses, Fannie decided.

"How is it you call her Miss Jane?" Myrtle asked.

"She didn't want to be called Mrs. Locke, and it's not fitting for servants to call her by her first name."

"She seems a good sort."

Fannie nodded. "She is." *Unlike Miss Harriet.*

She decided to keep mum about Miss Harriet's disposition. Myrtle would find out soon enough that Miss Jane and Miss Harriet were as different as day and night. And there was no need to tell her that nine years ago Miss Jane was down and out and sick with shock over her husband's death, and Miss Harriet took her in.

Fannie remembered being surprised, at the time, that Miss Harriet would do something kind. She knew, now, that kindness had nothing to do with it. Miss Harriet had seen an opportunity and grabbed it. Not only did Miss Jane arrange all Miss Harriet's appointments and keep track of her social engagements and supervise the running of the house—she filled in whenever a servant quit, which was often.

Fannie suppressed a sigh. Everything changed after old Mrs. Hunterdon died and Miss Harriet took over. She would have quit, but she'd served Miss Harriet's parents since Miss Harriet and her brother Mr. Alistair were children. She decided she was too old to start over in a new place. She was used to Miss Harriet's sharp tongue and mean ways. She could put up with it for the years she had left.

Miss Harriet talked even worse to Miss Jane than she did to the servants. Fannie often wondered why Miss Jane stuck around. She should have recovered from the shock of her husband's death long ago and being a registered nurse, she could have gotten a job, any time. For some reason, she stayed. It wasn't that Miss Jane was fond of Miss Harriet, Fannie thought. More than a few times she'd overheard the two of them having words and Miss Harriet saying to Miss Jane, "Go ahead, move out and see what happens!" But Miss Jane stayed on and put up with her.

With this last thought, Fannie decided she'd answered enough of Myrtle's questions. Let her find things out for herself.

*   *   *

Harriet Hunterdon Zanardi stood in her lavishly marbled and mirrored bathroom, frowning at her reflection and longing for a cigarette. She'd never had bulges around her waist till she gave up smoking. She wanted to say, "To hell with Dr. Finley", and send Jane out for a carton of Camels, but he'd scared the daylights out of her with his lecture about lung cancer running in the family. Too late, she'd realized what reaching for a sweet instead of smoke would do to her figure.

But her waist bulges weren't the only cause for frowning. She was losing the looks that had established her as a debutante, and glamour girl of Manhattan's society. Her blond hair now needed constant touchups against the onslaught of gray, and she was developing wrinkles too. That furrow between her eyes made her look like her great grandmother for whom she was named, whose portrait hung over the fireplace in the library. Well, two failed marriages were enough to make anyone frown. After she got tired of Paolo playing around and divorced him, she'd given up on marriage. In one respect, the men who'd been in and out of her life were all alike. They were after the Hunterdon money. She sighed; remembering she'd once believed Gus and Paolo would have married her without it.

Regretful thoughts crowded her mind. She was pushing sixty and what did she have to show for it? She was without husband or children and virtually without family. She and her younger brother, Alistair, were the last of the Hunterdons, except for the two brats he'd spawned in England. But she and Alistair hadn't seen one another in years. They'd never gotten along, anyway. Alistair had always been spoiled rotten. He'd been their parents' favorite because he was the son they'd always wanted, born years after they'd resigned themselves to having just one child, a daughter. From the day of his birth, Alistair got all the attention.

She and Alistair had each been left a sizeable fortune by

their parents, apart from the bulk of the estate. When one of them died, their parents' estate would go to the survivor. They'd also inherited the house and all its furnishings jointly, with a stipulation. Whichever of them died first, the house would revert to the other. But soon after their mother died, Alistair had gone to England where he'd married some snooty British girl from the fringes of royalty. She suspected they'd been squandering his inheritance around Europe ever since.

A frown deepened the furrow between her eyes. She'd received word a few days ago that Alistair and his wife and their two sons were coming to live in New York, permanently. Of course they were going to move into the house. There was nothing she could do to stop them. The house was as much Alistair's as it was hers. That's the way it would be till one of them died.

Letting her retrospective thoughts continue, she had to admit that besides being almost without family, she was virtually friendless. To have friends you had to like people and you had to be nice to them. She'd never been any good at either.

There were only three people she might possibly call friends—the two men she'd discarded with generous financial settlements, plus the promise of more from her will if she died before they did, and Jane, whom she'd rescued from poverty and a mental collapse. Whether any of them thought of her as a friend, she neither knew nor cared. It only mattered that each one of them was useful to her.

She'd made sure her partings from Gus and Paolo were amicable. Her ex-husbands came in handy when she needed an escort to the theatre, charity events, dinners and parties. Especially Paolo, who fit into the social scene better than Gus.

Manhattan's leading hostesses invited her to their soirees—not because they liked her any better than she liked them, but because she'd continued to hold the traditional Hunterdon New Year's Day bash which harked back to the early days of her grandparents' marriage and had become a *must* on the social calendars of Manhattan's high society. They might hate her guts, but they had to reciprocate. Nobody wanted to risk being stricken from the Hunterdon Party list.

Gus had used some of his settlement to buy a farm in the horsey area of New Jersey, where he raised thoroughbreds. He'd become a country gentleman—a far cry from the beefy hunk, pro-football linebacker, Gus "Speedbump" Stanky, whom she'd married against her parents' wishes.

Gus' football career came to an abrupt end after a knee injury three years into their marriage. While he was playing football he was also playing the horses with every dime of his eight-figure salary. With that gone, and his TV commercials for deodorant soap cut off, he was flat broke. She was tired of him by that time, anyway. He wanted children. She didn't. Who needed years of sniveling and whining brats? Not to mention what even one pregnancy would do to her figure. Father was delighted to be rid of Gus and came up with a handsome settlement.

Paolo had purchased a Fifth Avenue condo and had become quite the man about town. He was still the swarthily-handsome hand-kisser she'd thrown out for womanizing. He continued to pass himself off as a Tuscan count, even though Father had the Hunterdon attorneys research Paolo's background and found out he came from several generations of goat herders. But nobody else had to know about that, especially the people who fawned over titles.

As for Jane, they'd never actually been friends, just acquaintances in college. But when she read in the newspaper about Jane's no-good husband being shot outside a sleazy bar and Jane left penniless, on the verge of a mental breakdown, she got in touch with her immediately and offered her a home.

She did it because she thought Jane would be useful to her, if only temporarily, acting as her social secretary and filling in when servants quit. She expected Jane to leave when she got over her shock. She didn't expect it to turn out the way it had. It was sheer luck, catching Jane at the lowest ebb of her life. In a sobbing litany of regret, Jane had blurted out a confidence which would keep her here as long as she was wanted.

The procession of thoughts had temporarily driven her craving for a smoke out of her mind. Now it returned, more intense than ever. She couldn't endure it any longer. Jane would have to go out and get cigarettes for her.

She called Jane's bedroom on the house phone. "I need cigarettes. Drop whatever you're doing and go out and get me a carton of Camels," she ordered.

"Have you forgotten what Dr. Finley said?" Jane asked, in the calm, sweet voice that always irritated Harriet.

Harriet retorted with an expletive regarding Dr. Finley.

Jane disregarded it. "You told me you knew you had to quit. You told me not to pay any attention to you when you asked me to get you cigarettes."

Twitching with the need for nicotine, Harriet shrieked into the phone. "Don't argue with me, you miserable old crone. If you're not back here with my smokes in half an hour, you'll be sorry."

"Calm down, Harriet. I'll call the kitchen and have Fannie make you a pot of herbal tea. Then I'm coming to your room to talk to you."

"I don't want any damn herbal tea," Harriet shouted, "and don't think you can talk me out of smoking, again. It won't work this time." But Jane had already hung up.

Jane better get her the cigarettes if she knew what was good for her, Harriet said to herself. When Jane thought it over, she'd go out for the smokes, all right. Meanwhile, when Fannie brought the tea, a stiff shot of vodka in it would tide her over.

She went to her nightstand and opened the cabinet where she always kept a bottle of her favorite booze. She liked to have it handy. She especially liked a couple of straight vodkas after she went to bed. No ice. That only diluted it.

Alistair used to jaw at her about her drinking. Not that he didn't hoist a few himself when he wanted to. But as he used to say, he was always a gentleman. His way of inferring that with booze under her belt she wasn't always a lady.

She grimaced, remembering that Alistair would soon be returning to New York with his English wife and the two Brit brats, and they'd be moving into the house. Having them underfoot all day, she'd need more than two vodkas at bedtime.

Waiting for Jane, and for Fannie to bring her the herbal tea, she took a swig from the bottle. The vodka left its warming trail, calming her nerves. A few moments later she had to admit she shouldn't go back to cigarettes. She sure as hell didn't want to get lung cancer. Before it killed her, it would finish off what was left of her looks.

When Jane showed up, she'd tell her to forget about going out for the Camels. But the bottle should be stashed out of sight, or Jane might deliver a sermon about drinking. Jane never knew how close her preaching brought her to being smacked in her holier-than-thou face. But slapping Jane would destroy the last shred of harmony that still existed between them. Things were bad enough. No use making them worse. She took another swig from the bottle, then put it back into the cabinet.

Her hand brushed against something in a corner of the cabinet. It felt like . . . yes, it was, a pack of Camels, almost full, and a book of matches. She must have put them in there and forgotten them. What a time for cigarettes to turn up, after what she'd just gone through. They were probably staler than a Bill Clinton joke, but a few minutes ago she'd have smoked one anyway.

Jane's knock sounded on the door. She shoved the cigarettes and matches back into the cabinet. When she got desperate for a smoke again, stale or not, she'd know where to look.

Chapter One

Manhattan, two weeks later

Liz Rooney turned off her alarm clock and reached for the TV remote control. She always liked to catch the early morning news before getting out of her sofa bed. Today was Monday. A sensational murder could have happened during the night. Homicides seemed to occur more frequently on weekends. She had a passion for following murder cases, the more sensational the better. Not only following them, but trying to solve them.

A news broadcast had just started. Anything for her amateur sleuthing to latch onto would be in the lead story. There wasn't. The female newscaster finished a brief announcement of a flamboyant showbiz couple's split up, then, looking properly grave, reported on the accidental death of a Manhattan socialite.

"Countess Harriet Hunterdon Zanardi, member of one of New York's most socially prominent families, died last night of toxic smoke inhalation from a smoldering fire in her bedroom at the Hunterdon residence. Fire department spokesmen stated that the countess' brother, Alistair Hunterdon, was awakened by a smoke alarm and called 911.

"Firemen further stated that the fire, contained to the

10

countess' bedroom, was caused by a lit cigarette falling to the carpet and eventually igniting the skirt of an uphol- stered chair.

"According to paramedics, fumes from the smoldering upholstery were toxic enough to have caused the countess' death within a few minutes. Evidently a smoke alarm lo- cated in the hall outside the countess' bedroom did not waken her. By the time the fumes triggered a second smoke alarm at the opposite end of the bedroom hallway and alerted other household members, it was too late to revive the countess."

A photo of the countess flashed on, as the newscaster continued with more details, including her age, 58. The newscaster commented that the photo had been taken at a recent charity event.

The countess was a good-looking lady, Liz thought. She must have been a beauty in her younger days. Terrible, what happened to her. Smoking was bad enough in itself, but smoking in bed was asking for trouble.

Listening to the rest of the news, she went behind the screen to her kitchenette to start the coffeemaker. When the newscaster started to talk about baseball scores, she knew whatever homicides had occurred in the city last night weren't the sensational slayings involving the rich and fa- mous, which she loved to delve into. Most likely they in- volved punks or street gangs and were drug-related, and they'd happened in some hole-in-the-wall slum apartment or in an alley near a sleazy bar. Any mention of them in the news would be in the back pages of newspapers, if they were mentioned at all.

With no baffling murder case to challenge her wits, she left for work with nothing on her mind except her devel- oping relationship with Ike. What a difference a few weeks made! On the subway, she reviewed it all.

Until recently, she and NYPD Homicide Detective George Eichle called one another by their last names. He used to openly resent her interest in trying to solve homicide cases. If she showed up at a crime scene with her boss, Medical Examiner Dan Switzer, and Eichle was there, he'd gruffly ask, "What are you doing here, Rooney?"

When his attitude got too much for her, and she blew off a little steam, he made caustic references to her red hair and Irish temper. She and her best friend, rookie cop Sophie Pulaski, used to call him Detective Sourpuss behind his back.

Yet, even back then, she'd found him attractive. He was too rugged looking to be stereotypically handsome, but his tall, athletic build, his gray eyes and unruly thatch of sandy hair added up to one undeniably sexy male. Her grandmother said he looked like old movie star Gary Cooper. Now, in addition to liking Ike's looks, she'd grown to appreciate his intelligence and his terrific sense of humor.

They'd gone from Eichle and Rooney to Ike and Liz after she'd come up with clues that helped him solve two recent cases. When another of her clues was instrumental in wrapping up his last homicide, they'd progressed even further.

For the past couple of weeks, they'd been seeing each other almost every evening—and not just to talk about homicides. Now, when he made reference to her red hair or her Irish temper, he did so with a teasing smile, punctuated by one or more kisses. After last night, she felt as if they were hovering on the brink of something more.

On her way to her workstation, she passed Dan's office and saw him at his desk, reading the *New York Times*. She called "Good morning" to him; he motioned for her to come in.

Having a boss who was a close friend of her father's, and having a father who was a retired NYPD homicide detective had been a big help in following murder cases. The two of them had been encouraging her since she was a kid. Dan had offered her this job in his office when she graduated from college.

With Pop and Mom living in Florida, now, she missed

Pop's input into her amateur investigations, but she was lucky to have Dan's. And now that Ike's attitude had changed, she expected he'd let her in on the progress of his future sensational homicides.

"Good morning, Lizzie," Dan said. The smile on his round, affable face lessened as he glanced at the *Times* headline. "I guess you heard about the Countess Zanardi."

"Yes, I caught it on the TV news. What an awful way to die—choked by smoke. I wonder why she didn't hear the smoke alarm right outside her bedroom?"

"Apparently she was in too deep a sleep."

"Maybe she'd taken a sleeping pill?"

"More likely a few stiff drinks and she passed out," Dan said. "The autopsy will pick up whatever it was."

Liz was aware that some bereaved families did not want postmortems done on their loved ones. "No objections to the autopsy?" she asked.

"The forensic team reported that the countess' brother gave them a bad time about it," Dan replied. "He was strongly opposed to it. But, under certain circumstances, when a death is unattended an autopsy is mandatory by law."

Liz recalled what he'd said about the stiff drinks. "How come you think liquor will be found in her system?"

Dan smiled. "When I was fresh out of medical school and your pop was a rookie cop, Harriet Hunterdon was known as the Madcap Debutante. When she had a snootful, she'd do all sorts of crazy stunts. Once she rode off on a carriage horse in front of the Plaza, while the driver was taking a break."

Liz couldn't help laughing. "Sounds like she was a crazy kid. She must have been fun."

"A crazy kid, yes, but with a few drinks under her belt, she got belligerent as hell, and she had a mouth like a sewer."

"You knew her?"

"The only encounter I had with her was in the ER where

I was interning. She'd fallen down in the lobby of the Waldorf and broken her wrist. She was high as a kite. Being a cop, your pop had more contact with her than I. She was hauled into the station house regularly for being drunk and disorderly in public."

"But wasn't that a long time ago? Maybe she—"

"Stopped drinking? No. According to my cop friends, she was picked up for DWI several times over the years, She used to drive a BMW, but she finally lost her driver's license."

"How did she get around after that?" Liz asked. "Did she have a chauffeur?"

"Not a private chauffeur. According to the cops, she kept the BMW in the same limousine service garage she always did, but after she lost her license the garage provided a chauffeur whenever she called for the car to be brought around."

"Do you know how she got to be a countess?"

"Her second husband's a European count. Italian, I think. They're divorced now, but she hung onto the title."

"Did she divorce her first husband too?"

"Yeah. He was a linebacker with the Oakland Raiders."

"Any children with either of them?"

"No—and it's just as well."

Liz had to agree. "Smoking and drinking in bed wouldn't get her a nomination for Mother of the Year. Will you let me know what turns up in the autopsy?"

"Sure thing," Dan replied. "I should have the full report by Wednesday afternoon."

Sophie phoned during the morning. She said she and her partner were on a break in a doughnut shop.

"I suppose you heard about that high society dame dying in the fire. Some of the older cops at the station house remember her when she was a wild kid. You wouldn't believe some of the capers she pulled when she'd been drinking."

"Oh, yes I would," Liz replied. "Dan remembers her too, and he filled me in. According to him, her drinking didn't stop when she grew up."

"That's what I heard too," Sophie said. "She probably went to bed, smashed, and passed out with a cigarette in her hand." She paused. "How's it going with you and Ike?"

"Okay. He came over for dinner last night. I made chile. Gram's recipe."

"When are you seeing him again?"

"Wednesday night."

"Hey. Sounds like you two are getting pretty tight."

"We sure are tighter than we used to be."

"You're not going secretive on me, are you? You'd tell me if anything important happened, wouldn't you?"

"You know I would."

"Good. Well, I gotta go. Talk to you tomorrow."

Liz hung up the phone with a smile. She and Sophie had been best friends since first grade at Our Lady Queen of Peace School on Staten Island. They'd seen each other through the wild crushes of adolescence and the relationships during college and beyond. Now Sophie was engaged to be married. From the moment Sophie had fallen in love with NYPD Officer Ralph Perillo, she wanted Liz to fall in love too.

Had it happened between her and Ike? Actions were supposed to speak louder than words, but she couldn't be sure until she heard him say it. Like breaking away from calling her Rooney, she wanted him to be the instigator.

While passing by a newsstand on the way back from her lunch break, she noticed the *New York Post*'s bold headlines above a photo of Harriet Hunterdon Zanardi:

DEAD COUNTESS WAS MADCAP DEB

She picked up a copy. It would be interesting to read about the antics of debutante Harriet Hunterdon, she thought. On the elevator, she skimmed through the article. In addition to covering the countess' youthful escapades, her family background was fully described, dating back to ancestors who came over on the *Mayflower*.

Back at her desk, she continued reading the article. The countess' survivors were listed. She had a brother who'd been living in England and had come back to New York and moved into the Hunterdon residence with his wife and two sons only a week before the fire. "Alistair Hunterdon, brother of the countess, and his two sons Randolph and David, are the last of the Hunterdons," the article stated.

Liz was surprised to read the names of Count Paolo Zanardi and Gus "Speedbump" Stanky among the survivors. She didn't think it was customary for ex-husbands to be listed as survivors. Evidently the erstwhile Madcap Deb was not one to be dictated to by custom. She must have made it clear that when she died she wanted the news media to mention the count and the linebacker among her survivors.

Further proof of this was the inclusion of another non-relative on the list of survivors. "Mrs. Jane Locke, long-time friend of the countess, who has been living in the Hunterdon residence for the past nine years."

Though no emphasis had been put on the countess' drinking, enough was said in the article to portray her as someone who'd never be asked to join the Woman's Christian Temperance Union.

A real character, Liz thought. She put the newspaper aside and got to work.

On Wednesday, just before quitting time, Dan came to her desk. "I got the report on the Zanardi autopsy," he said.

From the look on his face, she sensed something unexpected had shown up. Sleeping pills in addition to alcohol, maybe? That combination could have killed her before the smoke did.

"So what put her into such a deep sleep?" she asked.

"Isopropanol," Dan replied. "It's similar to ethyl alcohol but twice as deadly. It can cause coma in a few minutes. It's a component in common household cleaning products."

From what Liz had learned about Harriet Hunterdon Zanardi's drinking habits, this didn't surprise her. The countess had probably been high on booze when she went to bed, and when she decided she needed one final swig, she could have mistaken a bottle of household cleaner for a bottle of liquor. "How could she take even one sip of something like that without noticing it smelled and tasted bad?" she asked.

"The amount of booze in her system indicates she was drunk when she went to bed," Dan replied. "She could have swilled down one last drink straight out of a bottle without even noticing the taste. Enough isopropanol was found in her blood to put her into a coma quickly. Eventually, it caused severe hemorrhaging in her trachea and bronchial tubes, as well as the chest cavity. Combined with the smoke she inhaled, she didn't have a chance."

"Sounds like there was more smoke than fire."

Dan nodded. "And evidently the carpet and chair upholstery were sized with formaldehyde. That would make the fumes toxic enough to kill her in a short time."

"So, she drank that iso . . . whatever it is, stuff, by mistake, while she was smoking in bed, and it knocked her out, and then she dropped her cigarette on the carpet?"

"Not exactly," Dan said. "At first we thought she was drunk enough to have picked up the wrong bottle, one containing a household cleaner, but it's more probable that the isopropanol was in her liquor bottle. Then, the final tests showed she hadn't been smoking that night. No trace of nicotine turned up in the autopsy."

Liz stared at him, her mind racing. "Are you saying someone spiked her booze and planted the cigarette?"

"Right. This death was no accident, Lizzie. It was deliberate murder."

Chapter Two

Murder! The word never failed to jolt her mind, bringing on the familiar excitement. Another sensational homicide to challenge her sleuthing talents!

"You'll have an interesting time with this one, Lizzie," Dan said, with an indulgent smile. "Sorry it wasn't established as a homicide right away so we could go to the scene. But the Hunterdon residence is in your detective friend's precinct. I've notified Homicide over there. If Ike goes on the case, he'll tell you what you want to know."

There was a good chance Ike and his partner Lou Sanchez would be assigned to this case, Liz thought, as she walked to the subway. If they were, they'd go over to the Hunterdon home immediately. That meant Ike would be late showing up at her apartment tonight. Well, they hadn't planned anything special—just dinner out somewhere and a movie afterwards. Anyway, instead of the movie, she'd rather return to her apartment after dinner and discuss the case. It was good, being on this new footing with Ike. No more trying to drag information out of him. Now, he respected her interest in following homicides and her investigative ability. Also, he'd told her the DA had been impressed when she came up with an important clue during the last big case, and now acknowledged her as a helpful citizen.

This was a little like being a detective herself, she thought, walking from the subway to her apartment building. Though she'd never considered entering police academy and going on to become a homicide detective, she and Sophie had often talked about forming their own private investigation firm some day.

Approaching her building, a nineteenth century house converted into four apartments, she saw the landlady, Rosa Moscaretti, at her kitchen window. They both smiled and waved.

Liz's smile lingered as she climbed the stairs to her apartment, directly above the Moscarettis'. She'd become too fond of Rosa to consider her nosey, but there was no denying that Rosa and her husband, Joe, kept track of their tenants' activities, especially hers. The Moscarettis had made friends with Mom and Pop when they went with her to look at the apartment. After she moved in, they'd assumed the roles of proxy parents. As Rosa put it, "a nice girl living alone in New York needs looking after."

Their vigil had waned since Ike began coming by, regularly. Liz was sure Rosa had decided if any male could be trusted, it would be that nice young cop.

She let herself into her apartment, pleased with the thought that everyone in her life liked Ike. The Moscarettis, Pop, Mom, Gram, Dan, even Sophie, now that she'd decided Ike wasn't Detective Sourpuss anymore, but a potential mate for her best friend.

Her thoughts returned to Dan's startling announcement. If Ike and Lou had been assigned to the case, they were probably at the Hunterdon residence right now. How long would it take to interview the servants and other members of the household? Her need for information was acute. To ward off her impatience, she sat down on the sofa and turned the TV to a news channel.

Evidently the news media had not yet been informed that

the supposed accidental death of Countess Zanardi was a homicide. She watched a brief rehash. Already, it was being relegated to secondary news status. But not for long. By tomorrow, the murder of the Madcap Debutante would make headlines in newspapers and dominate TV newscasts, all over again.

With Ike at the crime scene, there was no telling when he'd show up, she thought. She'd better think about putting something together for dinner in.

A check of her fridge and freezer proved to be discouraging. Three shriveled franks and a bowlful of leftover beans wouldn't hack it. But that frozen dab of chopped beef might be whipped up into something. Spaghetti, maybe? A look through her cabinet came up with the pasta, but no sauce.

Just as she'd decided they'd have to go out to eat, after all, the mouth-watering aroma of made-from-scratch Italian tomato sauce rose from the Moscarettis' kitchen. She rushed to the phone.

"Rosa?"

"Yes. Is that you, Liz, dearie? Is something wrong?"

"Nothing's wrong, except Ike's coming over for dinner and I want to make spaghetti but I forgot I was out of sauce and didn't buy any last time I went to the market. Could you possibly spare some of yours?"

Rosa's voice couldn't have been more disapproving if Liz had said she was out of arsenic. "You were going to feed that nice young cop sauce out of a jar?"

Liz had just come back to her apartment with a bowlful of Rosa's sauce, plus half a loaf of crusty Italian bread and a dish of freshly grated Romano cheese, when the phone rang.

That's probably Ike saying he'd be late, she thought. It was.

"Hello, Ike. I guess you're calling from the Hunterdon place."

"Right. So Dan told you the accidental death turned out to be a homicide?"

"Yes. I suppose you'll be tied up over there for a while."

"Yeah. Sorry. I'll get there soon as I can. Maybe another hour."

"Don't worry about it. We'll eat in. I'll make spaghetti."

"Sounds good. I'll pick up a bottle of Chianti on the way."

At 7:30, she put the sauce to heat in the microwave. By the time Ike got there a few minutes later, the mouth-watering aroma of Rosa's spaghetti sauce pervaded the apartment.

"That smells great. Are you sure you don't have a few Italian genes?" he asked, giving her a hug.

"Nope," Liz replied, with a laugh. "I'm Irish, all the way. The sauce is Rosa's."

They took their plates to the gateleg table she set up when someone came for dinner. When she ate alone, she took a tray and sat on the sofa. Lately, the gateleg table had been getting a workout. She might as well keep it open all the time. Thinking about future meals with Ike gave her a good feeling.

They'd have plenty of opportunity to discuss this latest homicide, she thought, as she watched Ike pour the wine. No more frustrating waits for him to let her in on developments.

"So, how did it go at the Hunterdon house?" she asked, eager to get going on her own sleuthing.

He took a swallow of wine before replying. "This is going to be a tough one."

She waited for him to continue. He didn't. Instead, he tasted a forkful of spaghetti. "Mmmm," he said. "It's obvious Mrs. Moscaretti is *Italian* all the way."

The evasion was reminiscent of his former attitude, she thought. "So it's going to be a tough case. Is that all you have to tell me?" she asked.

"There's not a hell of a lot to tell, yet."

"Didn't you interview the servants and the family?"

"Sure."

"You must have formed some opinions."

"We didn't come up with any one particular suspect, if that's what you mean."

He was starting to sound like Detective Sourpuss. "Aren't you going to let me in on anything?" she asked.

He took another forkful of spaghetti. "Well, one thing Lou and I both picked up. The countess is the least mourned victim of any homicide case we've ever investigated. There wasn't a red eye in the house, even after we announced her death wasn't accidental."

"Not even her brother?"

"I got the impression there'd been no love lost between them."

"What about that woman, Mrs. Jane Locke? She's been living there for years. She and the countess must have been close friends."

"She didn't come across as grieving either."

"And the servants?"

"We got the same impression."

He seemed to be loosening up, but he still had a long way to go, Liz thought. She wanted more details. "How many servants do they have?" she asked.

"Two. The cook's only been there a couple of weeks, so it wasn't unusual for her to be unaffected by what happened. But the other one—an elderly maid—she told me she worked for the Hunterdons since the countess and her brother were children, and yet she didn't appear to be as upset and saddened as you'd expect."

"Only two servants? You'd think such a wealthy home would have more than that," Liz said.

Ike nodded. "When I interviewed the elderly maid, she told me the countess had trouble keeping help. She said they'd been trying to get another maid for almost two months. She said the last one quit after a row with the countess."

Someone in that household disliked the countess enough to want her dead, Liz thought. Of course Ike realized this too. Why hadn't he said so? Why hadn't he described the members of the household to her, so they could kick some ideas around?

As if he sensed her annoyance, he took a quaff of wine and looked at her with the suggestion of a frown. "It's too soon to speculate, Liz."

"Don't you have any idea what the motive was?"

"Not yet."

"Are you going to contact the Hunterdon attorneys to see who's on the beneficiary list?" she asked. "The combination of disliking the countess intensely and knowing her will might make you rich, would be a strong motive."

"Right," he replied. "But what do you say we knock off talking about the case and just enjoy this great meal? Thanks for deciding not to eat out. This way I can relax. It's been a long day."

He is shutting me out. She'd anticipated discussing the motive and possible suspects, but they'd barely scratched the surface.

He hadn't told her who was in the house on Sunday night, before the countess went to bed and swilled her last drink of vodka. The brother and his family had probably been there, and the countess' friend, Jane Locke. Most likely the servants had Sunday off.

And what about the countess' two ex-husbands? She was friendly enough with them to want them listed as survivors, so maybe they were there Sunday night. Maybe the countess had thrown a dinner party and they were included. If that were so, then maybe the servants weren't off. They could have swapped Sunday for another day off. Ike should be letting her in on all this. It seemed as if they were back to taciturn detective and nosey civilian.

If Ike had any idea what was fomenting in her mind, he didn't let it affect his appetite. He polished off his spaghetti and inquired about chances for a refill.

"Sure, there's plenty left," Liz said, taking his plate. Behind the kitchenette screen, she let her thoughts develop. Ike must have decided he'd overstepped by letting her in on unannounced police information. Maybe he believed he'd been influenced by their growing relationship and decided not to tell her as much, from now on. But why would he decide that? He'd told her the DA valued her input.

A possible answer flashed into her mind. Was Ike in line for a promotion? As the daughter of a NYPD detective, she knew all about petty politics within the department. Did Ike think someone might try and block the promotion if he or she knew he'd shared confidential police information with a civilian?

This seemed out of character for Ike, but she couldn't rule it out. She knew she had to think of another way to delve into the death of Countess Harriet Hunterdon Zanardi. The mechanics of her mind went into full gear.

"You're very quiet all of a sudden," Ike said. "Is it because I didn't tell you enough about my interviews?"

"Nothing like that. I was thinking about my grandmother. She hasn't been feeling well."

Two lies, the last one a biggie. First, she hadn't been thinking about Gram. Second, when she'd talked to Gram on the phone the day before yesterday, Gram had just returned from a bus trip to Atlantic City with her ladies church group. She'd won $75 playing slot machines and planned to spend it on a new outfit for the next senior citizens dance.

"I'm sorry to hear she's not up to par," Ike replied.

She only half heard him. No sooner had she spoken the lies about Gram when she thought of a way she could investigate the countess' murder herself. It was a daring plan. Before she got too far into it, she'd give Ike one more chance. Maybe, after dessert and coffee, he'd loosen up.

"I have vanilla ice cream for dessert," she said, when he'd finished his spaghetti refill. "And some chocolate stuff to put on it, if you'd like."

"Sounds great," he said.

They had dessert, then carried their coffee to the sofa.

"Does the news media know the countess' death wasn't accidental?" Liz asked, turning on the TV.

"That information should have been released by now." He flashed her a grin. "Thanks to Dan, you knew about it before they did."

He was excusing himself for not giving her any information himself, she thought. Not only that, but it looked as if he had no intention of telling her anything about this case before the media was informed.

They watched a news program and listened to a revised report on the countess' death.

"Police say the death of Countess Harriet Hunterdon Zanardi, first believed to be accidental, has now been declared a homicide," the newscaster announced. He went on to say the autopsy showed no trace of nicotine, indicating that the countess had not been smoking. "Police now say that the cigarette found smoldering next to the bed had not fallen from the countess' hand but had been deliberately pressed into the carpet." He advised viewers to stay tuned for further developments. Liz was surprised that there'd been no mention of the toxic substance found in the countess' system.

"I knew Dan must have told you the countess hadn't been smoking," Ike said.

This was to excuse why you hadn't told me yourself.

"Yes, and he also told me they found something in her system that caused her to go into a coma," she replied.

"I figured he had," Ike said.

She held back an exasperated sigh. This was like saying there was no need for him to let her in on anything because Dan had already informed her. She tried another tack. "Was there a glass on her nightstand?"

He shook his head. "No glass."

Dan was right, Liz thought. The countess' last drink had come straight from a bottle—a booze bottle laced with a toxic substance. And of course no bottle was found in the countess' room. The killer would have removed it and gotten rid of it. Ike knew this. He was being a real pain.

Perhaps sensing her annoyance, he came through with a crumb of information. "It was three days before the countess' bedroom was considered a crime scene. We thought a glass might have been removed. But Fannie the maid said she didn't find a glass when she cleaned the bedroom after the body was taken to the morgue." With an air of finality, he picked up his mug and took a swallow of coffee.

No mention of the missing bottle. If this next-to-nothing information was all he planned to tell her, he'd had his chance and he'd blown it. It was time to get going on her plan.

She waited till he'd finished his coffee. "I know you have a busy day tomorrow," she said.

"That sounds like you're throwing me out," he said with a grin.

"I know you have a lot more digging to do at the Hunterdon house, that's all."

"Right, we do." He set his coffee mug on a nearby table and took her hand. "It's been a while since I pulled an eat-and-run, Liz."

It had, she thought. For the past couple of weeks they'd been watching movies after dinner. There'd been kissing and snuggling, too, a little more each time he came over. There'd be none of that, tonight. This was just as well, she told herself. Another evening like the last one would only remind her where they were inevitably heading, and make her wonder, again, when he'd mention the L word.

At the door, he gave her a light kiss. "I'll call you tomorrow," he said.

She gave him a hug and said goodnight.

As she listened to his footsteps descending the stairs, her half-formulated plan rushed to the forefront of her mind. It was ironic that Ike, with his sparse information, had unwittingly provided her with enough details to carry out her scheme.

She knew exactly what she was going to do and how she was going to do it.

Chapter Three

Lying in bed, Liz let it all come together in her mind. She recalled what little information Ike had told her. The Hunterdon household was shy a maid, he'd said. The countess had trouble keeping servants. They'd been trying for a couple of months to get another maid.

The need must be especially urgent now that the countess' brother, Alistair, and his wife and sons were living there, she thought. This made her plan workable.

Today was Wednesday. On her lunch break tomorrow, she'd go to an employment agency that provided domestic help for Manhattan's wealthiest households. She'd pose as someone seeking a job as a live-in housemaid. If all went well, by Friday night she'd be settled into the servants' quarters at the Hunterdon residence.

Monday was the Memorial Day holiday. That would give her three full days to snoop around, to become acquainted with the other servants and size up Mr. and Mrs. Alistair Hunterdon and Mrs. Jane Locke—maybe even the two ex-husbands. They'd probably be hanging around, offering their condolences.

Making sure she was sent to the Hunterdon home and not some other place might present a glitch in her plan. But maybe she'd be given a choice. She wouldn't know till she got to the employment agency.

The agency wouldn't send her out without a reference. No problem. She'd say she'd been employed by an elderly lady on Staten Island. *And the elderly lady would be Gram!*

She smiled imagining Gram's reaction. She'd go for the plan one hundred percent. Passed along with Gram's red hair and blue-green eyes was their mutual interest in following homicides. They'd work together to put the plan into action.

She went to the phone and called Gram. As expected, the entire subterfuge delighted her. "But we need to go over the details very carefully." Gram said. "I think you should come and spend tomorrow night with me so we can talk this over and head off any possible problems."

"Good idea," Liz replied. "I'll take a bag to work with me tomorrow morning and leave directly from there for the ferry."

It would seem like old times, getting to work the next morning via the eight o'clock boat from Staten Island. She'd done this for almost a year, before Pop retired from the force and he and Mom sold the New Dorp house and moved to Florida.

Gram was waiting on the front porch of her house when Liz walked along the tree-lined street on her way from the New Dorp train station. She waved. Liz waved back.

What a neat grandmother, she thought. Besides her wonderful spirit, she'd kept herself a trim size twelve, and as long as she could make it down New Dorp Lane to Mr. Nicky, she'd always have her red hair.

"Dinner's ready," Gram said, as they hugged. "Beef stew. I know it's one of your favorites, and it's something you probably wouldn't make for yourself."

Liz gave an appreciative sigh as they went into the house. "It smells so good, and you're right, beef stew's something I wouldn't make for myself." But maybe she should get Gram's recipe and make it for Ike, she thought, before remembering how tight-mouthed he'd been last night. No beef stew for him till he loosened up.

They ate at the big, round table in the center of the spacious kitchen. Liz had always loved Gram's kitchen, with its old-fashioned glassed-door cabinets and huge porcelain sink on legs. It looked much the same as it did when she was a child. Grandpa's rocking chair still stood near the window overlooking the backyard. In her mind's eye, Liz could see him sitting there, smoking his pipe, reading the newspaper.

"Now, let's talk about your plan to infiltrate the crime premises," Gram said. "When are you going to the employment agency?"

"Tomorrow, on my lunch break."

Gram eyed Liz's gray linen-look pants suit and black and white checked shirt she'd bought on sale at Bergdorf's. "That snappy outfit won't do at all," she said. "Not that servant girls can't look fashionable, but when you go to the employment agency you want to look one hundred percent believable."

"I'm not going to wear this to the employment agency," Liz replied. "I packed a dark blue skirt and plain white blouse for tomorrow, and a blue cardigan sweater."

"Good," Gram said. Her eyes shifted to Liz's black sandals. "Those shoes won't do, either."

"I packed an old pair of walking shoes too."

Gram nodded approval. "You'll need comfortable shoes on the job," she said. "But you should do something with your hair. It looks too glamorous, curling around your shoulders like that. Better tie it back. I have an old barrette you can use."

"Glamorous? Thanks, Gram." Even while she laughed, Liz couldn't hold back a thought. Did Ike think her hair looked glamorous? He'd never said it was anything but red.

Liz was surprised when Gram suddenly asked, "Are you still seeing that detective your father likes so much?"

She tried to sound casual. "Ike? Sure. We get together now and then." And if he didn't start shaping up in the information department, it could get to be mostly *then*, she thought.

Gram gave her a searching look. "I know you dug up some important clues for him during his last couple of investigations. I got the impression he let you in on developments. Have you told him you're going undercover on this one?"

"No, I haven't. You might as well know it, Gram. I came up with this plan because he won't open his mouth about this new homicide. I don't understand why he suddenly clammed up."

"Liz, you're the daughter of a homicide detective. You know how that works."

"Sure I do, but with Ike and me it was different. At least I thought it was. After I helped him, he made me feel as if we were working together. Now all of a sudden everything's changed. You know how I am, Gram. I'm not going to wait around till he decides to toss me a few crumbs of information."

"He's not going to like this plan of yours," Gram said.

"I'm not going to tell him," Liz replied.

"What if he comes to the Hunterdon house unexpectedly and finds you there?"

"By the time I get there, he'll have finished his interviewing."

Gram shook her head. "I don't think you should count on him not coming back for more questioning."

"Are you trying to discourage me, Gram?"

"Not at all. I just want you to be prepared."

"I'll stay alert. If he does come back, I'll duck out of sight. There's no reason why he'd want to question a servant who didn't come to work there till five days after the murder."

"Maybe you're right," Gram said. "Now let's get on with your plan. You'll have to give your correct Social Security number and real name to the employment agency, but Elizabeth sounds too formal for a housemaid. At the Hunterdon house, you should have them call you something else, but something that ties in with the name on your Social Security card—your middle name, maybe, but I think a nickname for Elizabeth would be better than Anne. Liz is out, of course."

"Why?"

"If Ike comes back for more questioning, you don't want to risk someone mentioning a new maid named Liz."

Liz nodded. Gram was sharp as a tack. "Okay. How about Bette, or Bess or Beth?"

"Beth sounds all right to me."

"Then Beth it is. Do I have to worry about Rooney being mentioned in front of Ike?"

"No," Gram said. "In high society homes, most female servants might just as well not have last names and male servants might just as well not have first names."

Gram knew what she was talking about. Her grandmother emigrated from Ireland during the late 1800s and worked for several years as a parlor maid for wealthy New Yorkers. Things hadn't changed much since then, Liz decided, recalling Wade, a guy she'd dated for a while last winter. His frequent references to Jenkins the butler, Helga the cook and Rosie the maid left no doubt that his family was rich. Nouveau riche, most likely. People with old money wouldn't talk about their servants. It was like bragging.

"I wonder what my duties will be," she said, picturing herself dusting heirloom furniture and priceless antique bibelots.

"That depends on how many they have on the staff." Gram replied. She rose from her chair. "After we do the dishes, we should get to work on your letter of reference."

They sat on Gram's old living room sofa with the flowered upholstery, and composed the letter.

"Let's say you worked for me for four years," Gram said. "Why are you looking for a new job? You shouldn't say I died. That would be too easy to check."

"You could be going into a nursing home," Liz suggested.

Gram thought for a moment. "Let's say I was having financial problems and decided I had to cut down on expenses. That way you'll have an excuse to quit after your three days. You can tell them you phoned me to see how I was getting along, and I told you I changed my mind."

"You couldn't get along without me," Liz said, with a laugh. "You'll find a way to work me into your budget, somehow." She paused, "But won't I be expected to give two weeks notice?"

"Unless you have a contract, there's no law that says you can't quit a job whenever you want to."

Liz gave her a hug. "You think of everything, Gram. I couldn't pull this off without you."

Gram looked at her with a sigh.

"What's the matter? Are you having second thoughts about this?" Liz asked. "Don't you think I'll be a convincing housemaid?"

"Oh, it's not anything like that," Gram replied. "You've seen enough old TV movies to know how a servant is supposed to behave. I know you'll be 'yes ma'am-ing' and 'yes sir-ing' all over the place. I'm concerned about you and your cop friend. If he runs into you at the Hunterdon house, it could ruin whatever you have between you."

What *did* she and Ike have between them? Liz asked herself. After last night, she wasn't sure they weren't back to square one. If he caught her at the Hunterdon house it could be "What are you doing here, Rooney?" all over again.

But she wasn't going to drop the plan. "I'll just have to take my chances," she said.

The next morning, after reminding Liz she had a strenuous day ahead, and insisting she eat a hearty breakfast,

Gram sent her off to work. Standing on the front porch in her bathrobe, Gram wished her good luck.

"I'll phone you later today to let you know how it went at the employment agency," Liz said.

Boarding the train, she caught sight of her reflection in a window. For an instant, the young woman wearing a plain blouse and skirt and an old cardigan sweater looked like a stranger. There'd be some raised eyebrows when she appeared at work. Not that she was any kind of fashion plate, but she managed to maintain some degree of chic. Grandpa used to call the type of shoes she had on brogues. That was the Irish word for heavy, Oxford-style shoes. Hers were left over from her college days.

So as not to cause even more curiosity at work, she'd left her hair loose. Just before her lunch break she'd pull it back off her face, fasten it into a too-short ponytail, and be on her way to the employment agency.

She and Gram had looked in the Manhattan phone book and chosen an agency. Its ad said: Providing Manhattan's finest homes with superior domestic help since 1919. They'd both thought it sounded like an agency the Hunterdons might have been using for generations. Anyway, if the household's need for another maid was acute enough, every domestic agency in the city might have been contacted.

There were only a few applicants waiting to be interviewed when Liz got to the agency. An elderly woman at the front desk gave her a form to fill out. "When you've completed this, please return it to me with any letters of reference you have. Someone will interview you in a few minutes," she said.

A feeling of uncertainty came over Liz as she began to fill out the application. What if they sent some other woman to the Hunterdon home for the job and she was hired? Furtively, she eyed the handful of people waiting to be interviewed. A middle-aged man who could have played a British butler in an old movie, and a buxom, gray-haired woman who had all the earmarks of a cook. No competition there. She glanced at the others. Two men, one Asian, one black. Butlers? Chauffeurs? Gentlemen's gentlemen? A fortyish, Mary Poppins-type. None of them looked like an applicant for a housemaid job. But maybe a maid was being interviewed in one of those cubicles. Still feeling uncertain, she completed her form and handed it in, along with the reference letter.

While waiting for her name to be called, she watched applicants emerging from various cubicles and leaving the agency, calling cheery good-byes to the woman at the desk. They were going out to some of Manhattan's finest homes, as mentioned in the ad, Liz decided. One of them looked as if she might be a maid. About fifty, Liz judged. That meant she had experience—most likely on the staff in some high society home, not working as a lone, general maid for an elderly lady on Staten Island. If this mature, experienced woman was on her way to the Hunterdon home . . .

"Miss Rooney."

Liz came out of her thoughts with a start. The woman at the desk was motioning towards one of the cubicles, saying, "Mr. Weiner will see you now."

The middle-aged man behind the desk greeted her with a smile. "Sit down, Miss Rooney." he said. In his hands, he had her application and the glowing letter she and Gram had composed.

"Mrs. McGowan seems very sorry she had to let you go."

"Yes, sir," Liz replied. "We got along fine, Mrs. McGowan and me. I liked working for her." She put on an appropriately sad look. "I wish I didn't have to leave."

Mr. Weiner glanced at the letter again, then looked up to appraise her. "You're very young."

"I went to work for Mrs. McGowan right out of high

school," Liz said, hoping he hadn't started running a check of her record at New Dorp High. If he found out she'd gone on to Wagner College, her plan was doomed.

Mr. Weiner cast her a penetrating look. Her heart sank. Had he sensed something phony about her? Maybe he thought she was an investigative reporter for some newspaper, out to explore unethical practices of domestic employment agencies—if there were any to explore.

His smile dispersed her misgivings. "There's an opening for a maid in a fine, top-class home. You haven't had experience in this kind of home, but your reference is excellent, and these people need someone as soon as possible. I'm sure you'll fit in. I'll call now and set up your interview."

Before picking up his phone, he wrote something on a card and handed it to her. Relief flooded over her when she saw the name Mrs. Locke, followed by an address.

His phone conversation was brief. "Good news, Mrs. Locke. We have an applicant for a maid's job—a very personable young woman with an excellent reference. And she's a high school graduate."

Mrs. Locke must have jumped at the bait. He hung up the phone with a smile.

"You can go right over there," he said. "Mrs. Locke said they've just finished lunch and she'll be expecting you. Go to the service entrance."

Go right over there? She had to get back to work by 1:30. She hadn't had any lunch. She was hungry.

He must have noticed her distress. "Something wrong, Miss Rooney?"

"No," she lied. She'd just have to phone Dan and ask him if she could take a longer lunch break, she decided. She'd tell him she'd make it up by working beyond quitting time today.

She called him from a pay phone. "Sure, Lizzie, take whatever time you need," Dan said.

She grabbed a hot dog and coffee from a street vendor

and hailed a cab. When she gave the driver the Hunterdon address, she thought she might be out of character, arriving in a taxi. What if Mrs. Locke or one of the servants happened to be looking out a window and saw her? No use arousing suspicions. She asked the driver to let her out down the block.

Now she stood in front of a towering stone house—the kind built in Manhattan during the late nineteenth or early twentieth century. A short flight of concrete steps with highly-polished brass railings led to a massive double-door entrance flanked by flower boxes filled with pink geraniums. Doorknobs, knocker and mail slot were also buffed to a gleaming polish, she noticed. Would she be required to keep all that brass shining, she wondered. That would really do a number on her nails.

To the left of the main entrance, she saw a low iron fence with a gate and a few steps leading down towards a pair of grilled windows and a door. This must be the service entrance, she decided.

Well, this is it, Beth Rooney, she told herself. She went down the steps to the door and rang the bell.

Chapter Four

At first she thought the dark-skinned woman who answered the door might be Mrs. Locke. She changed her mind in a few seconds. The late Countess Zanardi's longtime friend wouldn't be wearing a black dress with white collar and cuffs and white apron. All that was missing from the traditional maid's outfit she'd seen in so many old movies, was the perky little cap.

Besides, she thought this woman looked too elderly to be the countess' contemporary. Her observations proved right.

"Come in," the woman said, swinging the door open. "I guess you're the maid the agency sent over. I'm Fannie. I've been a maid here for a good many years."

"Yes, I'm Beth," Liz said, following her into a huge kitchen that could have been the set for the British TV show, "Upstairs, Downstairs."

"Have a seat," Fannie said, motioning toward chairs at a kitchen table even bigger than Gram's. "I'll phone Miss Jane's room and let her know you're here."

Miss Jane. That sounded as if Mrs. Locke might be friendly with the servants, and evidently this house was so big that the occupants had to keep in touch by intercom.

As she watched Fannie go to a phone on the wall next

to the refrigerator, she noticed the refrigerator was one of those pricey, new, double-door, armoire models with a freezer on the bottom. She looked around for the stove and found it on the opposite wall. It looked new, too, and definitely top of the line. She located the sink. It looked like Gram's. She couldn't decide if it was as old as Gram's or if it was a brand new replica, now favored by kitchen designers. She noticed a new looking dishwasher next to it. Since this was a basement kitchen, there had to be a dumbwaiter to take the food up to a serving pantry near the dining room. She located it next to the stove.

Not exactly "Upstairs, Downstairs," but not *Home and Garden,* either.

When Fannie returned from the phone, saying Miss Jane would be right down, another woman appeared from a corridor off the kitchen. Liz had a first impression of graying, straw-colored hair and watery blue eyes, plus almost two hundred pounds of flesh squeezed into a white uniform topped by an oversized apron.

The woman scrutinized Liz. Her voice matched her curt manner. "I take it you're the new chambermaid."

Chambermaid. That sounded as if she'd be making beds and cleaning bathrooms, Liz thought.

"Not yet. I'm applying for the job," she replied.

"Beth, this here's Myrtle." Fannie said. "She's our cook."

The fat woman gave a sniff. "Cook and everything else too," She paused to glare at Liz. "You better take this job, Missy." With that, she turned and waddled back down the corridor.

Fannie gave a shrug. "She's cranky because she has to help with the upstairs work till we get someone. She thinks she's too good for that because in England she cooked for titled families and once even the Prince of Wales. She had a row with the countess about it. She was ready to quit, but Miss Jane talked her out of it."

A door at the top of the stairway opened. "Here's Miss

Jane now," Fannie said. "Miss Jane—this is the maid Mr. Weiner sent over. I'll go to my room so you can talk." She scurried down the same corridor where the cook had gone.

A slim, dark-haired woman, wearing tan slacks and a white, short-sleeved cotton sweater descended the stairs. Good looking, mid-fifties, with a smile that put Liz at ease.

"Hello," she said, walking across the kitchen, hand outstretched. "I'm Jane Locke. The agency said your name is Elizabeth Rooney."

Liz jumped to her feet. "Yes, ma'am, but I go by Beth."

"And around here, I go by Miss Jane," the woman said, with another smile. She seated herself at the table and motioned for Liz to sit down again. Her brown eyes studied Liz for a few moments. "You're not what I expected," she said.

Liz felt apprehensive. This sounded as if her ruse wasn't going to work.

Miss Jane's next words dispelled her fears. "You're young for this kind of job. Most women your age won't consider domestic work, especially high school graduates. But, according to Mr. Weiner, you finished high school and you've been working as a general maid."

"Yes, ma'am, I worked four years for a lady on Staten Island," Liz replied. She handed Miss Jane the letter she and Gram had composed.

Miss Jane read it. "An excellent reference," she said. "Mrs. McGowan regrets having to let you go."

"Yes, ma'am, we got along good. I wish I didn't have to leave, but Mrs. McGowan said she had to cut down her expenses."

Miss Jane glanced at the letter again. "She describes you as a willing worker. That's good. Although this opening is primarily for a chambermaid, we'd need you to assist in other areas such as helping to serve in the dining room."

"You said I'd be a chambermaid. What does that mean, exactly?" Liz asked.

"It means you'd keep the bedrooms and baths clean and

tidy and provided with whatever's needed. The bed linens
are changed on Saturdays and fresh towels put in the bathrooms every day. We have five bedrooms and four baths
upstairs. Three of the bedrooms have adjoining baths. The
other two share a bath."

The countess would have had one of the private baths,
Miss Jane another, and Alistair Hunterdon and his wife the
third, Liz decided. Their two sons shared the fourth bath.
A lot of people to clean up after.

"Who does the laundry?" she asked.

"You'd be helping Fannie with it." Miss Jane gestured
towards a door across the kitchen. "The washer and dryer
are in there." She paused. "We'd pay you the same wage
as Mrs. McGowan did." Again, she paused. "I think you'll
do very well here Beth. The job is yours if you want it."

This was almost too easy, Liz thought. They must be
desperate for help.

"Yes, ma'am, I want the job," she replied. She felt a
pang of guilt. On Monday she'd be telling Miss Jane she
was quitting.

"Good. I know you'll be just fine," Miss Jane said.
"Now, about uniforms. If you don't have your own, that's
all right. We have a number of them in the storeroom."
Again she gestured towards a door, this one at the foot of
the stairway. "We have all sizes. Fannie will show you
where they are. I'm sure you'll find some small enough to
fit you."

They must have built up quite an inventory what with
the big servant turnover, Liz thought. She held back a grin
as she pictured herself dressed as a housemaid.

"About your time off," Miss Jane continued. "After your
first week you'll have every Sunday off after breakfast, and
one other day a week after breakfast, according to our
needs. I'll see that you have a key to the service door. And
you needn't worry about setting off a burglar alarm by
mistake. We don't have one. A private neighborhood security guard patrols regularly."

Liz didn't want to appear meek and unsavvy. "Mrs. McGowan gave me all day Sunday off."

Miss Jane was silent for a few moments, probably picturing Sunday mornings with beds left unmade and bathrooms littered with soggy towels. "We have a late breakfast on Sundays," she said. "Our former chambermaids tended to the bedrooms and baths while the family was downstairs, eating. We'd like to keep that routine, so to compensate we'll offer you an increase in wages. Would ten dollars more per week be satisfactory?"

"Yes, ma'am," Liz replied. Again, she felt guilty. Miss Jane was a nice woman. She didn't deserve to be deceived like this.

"One more thing," Miss Jane said. "If you want to attend church on Sundays, you'll have plenty of time to go to an early service and get back here in time to do the bedrooms."

Liz nodded. "Yes, ma'am, I'll remember that." Miss Jane assumed she was Catholic because of her Irish name, she thought. No need to tell her she didn't go to mass every Sunday—she went just often enough to keep from being excommunicated.

"Let me show you your quarters," Miss Jane said. She led the way down the corridor where Fannie and Myrtle had gone, and opened a door.

Liz stared into a tiny room, furnished only with a bed, dresser and chair. Blinds were drawn over the lone window. She couldn't see what it looked out on, but she was sure there wasn't a breathtaking view.

"I know it looks very plain, but when you get your own things in here it will be quite cozy," Miss Jane said. "The bathroom's at the end of the hall. The servants take turns cleaning it. Each of you has white towels but with a different color border on the bottom. Fannie has a blue stripe and Myrtle has green. Yours will be pink."

Miss Jane certainly ran an orderly household, Liz thought, following her back to the kitchen. She wondered what she could bring from her apartment to make her room look as if she intended to stay.

"Now, how soon can you come, Beth?" Miss Jane asked. "We'd like you to be here by tomorrow night, if possible. We've had a death here and the funeral is Saturday afternoon."

Miss Jane must know she'd heard about the murder on the news, Liz thought. She should mention this and make an appropriate comment. "I heard about Countess Zanardi's death," she said. "Having such a terrible thing happen must be hard on you and everyone else in the house. I can be here about six on Friday evening, ma'am."

Miss Jane gave a grateful smile. "Oh, that's fine, Beth. We'll expect you around six tomorrow then."

Miss Jane didn't act like someone who'd planned the coma-and-smoke-inhalation, Liz thought, on her way back to the office. Neither did Fannie nor even high and mighty Myrtle. Besides, if one of them had done it, would she have stuck around? Wouldn't she have disappeared before the autopsy showed the death wasn't an accident? No, she decided. Disappearing would only make her the prime suspect. As far as she knew, nobody in the household had disappeared.

Back in her office, Liz found it difficult to keep her mind on her work. She wanted to call Gram, but didn't want her conversation to be overheard. Co-workers were already curious about her looking somewhat less than chic, today. They'd noticed her overnight bag too. She'd told them she'd spent the night with her grandmother. At least that much was the truth.

Tomorrow she'd come in wearing the same outfit, and with a larger suitcase and let it be known that her grandmother wasn't feeling well and she was going to spend the weekend with her. She knew there'd be comments such as, "You have to spend the holiday weekend with your grandmother? What a bummer." But Dan knew Gram. He'd ask concerned questions about her. She'd have to assure him it was nothing serious. She'd make something up—maybe that Gram had a touch of arthritis. She'd say she didn't have any special plans for the weekend, anyway and decided she might as well spend it making Gram feel more comfortable.

As soon as she got home, she phoned Gram with a full report.

"It sounds like everything's going smoothly," Gram said. "Did you pick up any ideas?"

"Not really. The cook thinks she's a cut above other servants because she used to work for British nobility. The maid's friendly, though. She told me she's worked there for a long time. I can't picture either of them committing a murder."

"And Mrs. Locke. How about her?"

"The servants call her Miss Jane. She's *very* nice. I can't imagine her having anything to do with the countess' death, either."

"I read in the paper the funeral's Saturday afternoon," Gram said. "The burial's going to be on Staten Island, in Moravian cemetery."

"That's almost in your back yard, Gram," Liz said. She remembered the New York Vanderbilt family had once lived on Staten Island, and they owned a large, gated section of Moravian cemetery with a huge mausoleum where generations of Vanderbilts were interred. "I guess the Hunterdons wanted to keep up with the Vanderbilts," she joked. "I wonder if *they* have a mausoleum too."

"I don't know, but I can find out," Gram said. "I'm going to take a walk over there Saturday. A high society funeral won't be hard to find. All those fancy cars. I'll check out whoever's at the gravesite and let you know what I picked up."

"Gram, you're a regular Miss Marple."

"We'll see," Gram said, with a laugh. "By the way, did you ever get a cell phone?"

"No. Pop wanted to give me one but I didn't think I'd use it enough."

"Get one and take it with you to the Hunterdons. We need to stay in touch while you're there."

"Okay, I'll buy one while I'm on my lunch break, tomorrow. And I'll call you tomorrow night."

After they said good-bye she wanted to phone Sophie and fill her in on what she was up to. But Sophie worked out of the same station house as Ike. She couldn't risk Sophie running into him and making some inadvertent remark. Her decision left her feeling bad. She and Sophie had never kept secrets from one another.

Mom and Pop always phoned her on Sunday nights. She called them, saying she was going away for the weekend. Another lie.

Ike phoned later. "I tried to get you a couple of times last night," he said.

"I was with Gram," she replied, trying to ignore the way the sound of his voice quickened her heart.

"I'm going to be tied up till pretty late, tonight, so maybe I shouldn't come over till tomorrow," he said.

"I'm going to be busy tomorrow night," she said. "Gram hasn't been feeling up to par and I'm spending the weekend with her." Lying to him made her feel rotten.

"Memorial Day too?" he asked.

"Yes." The idea that he might want to do something special with her on Memorial Day made her feel even worse.

"I hope it's nothing serious with your grandmother."

"No. She just needs to take it easy for a few days."

"Well, I guess we won't see each other till Tuesday," he said. "I'll call you at your grandmother's over the weekend."

"All right," she replied. Gram could always say she'd gone to the store, or something.

"We're definitely on for Tuesday night, aren't we?"

"Sure."

Like his facial expressions, Ike's voice never betrayed his feelings. She hung up the phone, wondering if he felt as down as she did.

Chapter Five

When Liz arrived in the Hunterdon kitchen a few minutes after six on Friday night, she found Fannie at the big table, cutting up salad ingredients. Cook pots bubbled on the range, serving dishes waited on a nearby cart, and Myrtle had just slammed the oven door shut. The delectable aroma of roasting lamb permeated the kitchen.

Fannie smiled and said hello. Liz returned the greeting.

"So you're here, are you?" Myrtle said. "It's about time. They're going to the funeral home for the viewing, so dinner's early tonight and we've two extra at the table. I want you to baste the roast right now, while I make the mint sauce."

"And hello to you too," Liz retorted. "You could at least give me a minute to take my bag to my room and wash my hands."

Myrtle stared at her. "A cheeky one, aren't you?"

"Only when called for," Liz replied. She headed down the corridor to the room Miss Jane had shown her. Myrtle's attitude was high and mighty, all right. Because she'd been a cook for British families with titles, she considered herself superior to American servants like Fannie—and Beth the new chambermaid. From Gram's stories about her immigrant grandmother, Liz knew domestic service had a caste system all its own.

In the bedroom, she opened the closet door and saw three maid's uniforms—two gray, one black. A pile of white aprons lay folded on the shelf. Fannie must have taken them out of the storeroom for her, she decided. Myrtle certainly hadn't.

"Thanks for putting the uniforms in my closet, Fannie," she said, when she returned to the kitchen.

"They look like they'll fit you," Fannie replied. "You can put one on after you're done with Myrtle's roast."

"Shall I wear the black or the gray?" Liz asked.

"The gray, and one of the fancy aprons. Miss Jane wants you to help me serve at the table tonight. There's company for dinner—the reverend and his wife."

Myrtle gave a loud snort. "While you're standing there chitchatting, me roast could be drying up. Get over here and start basting, Missy."

Liz choked off the urge to snap back at her. She recalled something Gram was fond of saying: "You can catch more flies with honey than with vinegar."

She walked over to the range and picked up the basting spoon. Opening the oven, she gave an exaggerated sniff. "Mmmm. Myrtle, this smells wonderful. Not everybody's good at doing a big roast. You must be a first-class cook."

Myrtle cast her a look, part-surprise, part-prideful. "Well, if I do say so meself, talk had it I was the best cook in London. In all of England, some said. All the titled swells was after me. When I served in Lord and Lady Gravistock's home, I once cooked dinner for the Prince of Wales."

Myrtle didn't say why or when she'd left England's noble kitchens to come to America, Liz thought, as she slathered drippings onto the roasting lamb. But Myrtle obviously had her standards. When she went to the New York employment agency looking for a job, she jumped at the chance to cook for a countess.

She recalled Fannie saying the countess and Myrtle had

a row when Myrtle balked at helping with the upstairs work. She was going to quit, Fannie said, but Miss Jane talked her into staying.

She spooned more drippings over the roast, letting her thoughts wander. It didn't appear as if Miss Jane had any plans to leave, even though her friend was dead. If the countess' brother planned to live in New York permanently, and he'd inherited the house after her death, maybe he'd persuaded Miss Jane to stay on as household manager.

Had the will been read yet? Whether or not it had, Ike must have found out, by now, who stood to benefit from it. Judging from his reluctance to let her in on anything the other night, she wasn't counting on getting any information from him about the beneficiaries. She might as well try and figure it out for herself.

Besides Alistair Hunterdon and his wife and sons, who else would there be? Fannie, who'd worked for the Hunterdons since the countess was a child? Miss Jane? She'd been a long-time, loyal friend. The countess' two ex-husbands? If she was on good enough terms with them to want them listed as survivors, she might also have provided for them in her will. It was possible she'd let all of them know they could expect a sizeable bequest when she died. Had greed been the motive for her murder?

Fannie and Miss Jane seemed too nice to have murdered the countess to get their bequests. And newcomer Myrtle wouldn't have been mentioned in the will at all, even if she hadn't had that big row with the countess. As for the other household members, she'd have to wait till she encountered them before she could make a judgment about them. But, whether they seemed nice or not, if any member of the household harbored a dislike for the countess, the prospect of sudden wealth might have been a strong motive.

Fannie's voice came into her thoughts. "The table's all laid and I'm done with the salad. I'm going to my room to change into my serving uniform."

Still mollified by the recent compliment about her cooking, Myrtle surprised Liz with a smile. "You get changed too. The mint sauce is near ready. I'll see to it and the roast, both."

Another compliment or two and I'll have Myrtle eating out of my hand!

The gray uniform fit. She added a ruffled white apron and surveyed herself in the dresser mirror, wishing Gram could see her.

Upstairs, in the serving pantry, she and Fannie unloaded the dumbwaiter. One glance into the dining room and Liz felt unsure of herself. Seven people at a table laid with a linen cutwork cloth and a centerpiece of fresh flowers flanked by silver candelabra. A dazzling array of silver knives, forks and spoons. Two stemmed crystal glasses at each place . . .

"I never served at a formal dinner before," Liz whispered.

Fannie gave a subdued chuckle. "You think this is formal? Tonight it's just Mr. Alistair and his family and Miss Jane and the reverend and his wife. Mr. Alistair's carving the roast himself, and we're not even using the best dishes."

"Oh?" Liz was surprised. In the kitchen, she had admired the dinnerware and inspected the bottom of a serving dish for markings. If antique Meissen wasn't the Hunterdon's best china, what was, she wondered.

"When Miss Harriet gave one of her formal dinners, we always used those white dishes in the dining room china cabinet, the ones with the fancy gold rims and the letter H," Fannie said. "They were a wedding present to her grandparents from President Theodore Roosevelt."

She gave Liz a reassuring pat on the arm. "Don't be nervous. Just remember, when we take the dishes round, always serve from the left, and when we clear, take the plates off from the right."

This was one thing she and Gram hadn't covered, Liz

thought. She managed to make the rounds without dropping or spilling anything. After everyone had been served, and she and Fannie watched and waited in the pantry, she did a bit of observing.

Alistair Hunterdon and his wife made a striking looking couple—he, lean and fit looking, with light brown, graying hair, good facial features and ruddy cheeks; she, slim and quite pretty, with a blond bob. Both looked to be in their late forties or early fifties. From the fragments of conversation, Liz deduced the wife's name was Sylvia. She couldn't imagine either of them committing murder.

Their two sons were older than Liz thought they'd be. One looked sixteen or seventeen and the other about nineteen. Good looking, blond, rosy-cheeked boys. They resembled their father. Again, from table talk, Liz gathered the younger one was David and the elder, Randolph.

She didn't spend any time observing the clergyman and his wife. Even if they'd been in the house on the night the countess was murdered, she believed she could safely disregard them as suspects.

She'd read in the newspaper that the funeral was to be held at St. Thomas' Episcopal Church tomorrow at 2 P.M. She remembered that Grandpa used to call Episcopalians God's frozen people. But hatred of the countess might have heated one of these frozen people to the boiling point.

"Time to go round with the serving dishes again," Fannie whispered.

Nobody except David and Randolph took second helpings. Randolph stared at Liz every time he scooped up his refill. She recognized the look. This kid had the rollicking hormones of a typical nineteen-year-old.

Dessert was lemon chiffon pie. Friends of the family had dropped two by, Fannie told her. "And the ice box is loaded with food folks sent over for after the funeral," she added. It gave Liz a good feeling to know this time-honored custom transcended social and economic classes.

Miss Jane's voice penetrated her thoughts. "I don't want to rush anyone," she said, looking around the table, "but we should be leaving for the viewing very soon."

Liz saw her smile at David and Randolph. "Sorry you boys won't have time for more pie." She glanced towards the serving pantry. "Maybe Fannie will put some aside for you and you can have it after we get back."

On cue, Fannie stepped out of the pantry. "Yes ma'am, I'll see to it."

Did that mean the boys would raid the fridge, Liz wondered. No, she decided. This wasn't a middle-class New Dorp house, or even a big, ritzy home in one of the hill sections of Staten Island. More than likely there'd be places set in the dining room and the pie served to them by Fannie.

Back in the kitchen, Myrtle was sitting at the table. While Liz and Fannie transferred the dinner dishes and silverware from dumbwaiter to dishwasher, she made no move to help.

"I already washed me pots," she announced, letting them know this was a British cook's sole cleanup responsibility. Another indication that cooking for titled English families had given her delusions of superiority.

Fannie uncovered the serving dishes. "We'll eat now," she said, taking clean plates out of the dish cabinet. Plain crockery, Liz noticed. Servants' dishes.

"Everything's gone cold by now, Beth," Myrtle said. "Fannie will warm up our food in the microwave."

Fannie frowned. "Did you think I'd let Beth eat cold food?" she snapped. "But I'm not waiting on you, Myrtle. You can heat your own food."

Fannie and Myrtle were always at odds, Liz thought. She hastened to head off the friction. "Whatever did we do before microwaves?" she asked.

She couldn't help noticing Myrtle's friendliness towards her. Her compliment about Myrtle's cooking had paid off, she thought. Good. She'd already planned to get information out of Fannie. With Myrtle getting chummy, maybe she could do the same with her.

When the three of them were seated at the table, eating, Liz included both Fannie and Myrtle in a remark she hoped sounded natural and sympathetic. "The countess' death, and the way she died, must have been an awful shock for you and everyone else."

Fannie nodded. "I knew her since she was a little girl."

"I've only been here a fortnight, so I can't rightly say I knew her at all," Myrtle said. "But from the little I seen of her, I can't say as I took any shine to her. She had a haughty way about her like she believed she was a real countess."

"You shouldn't speak ill of the dead," Fannie said.

Myrtle gave a snort. "You didn't like her, either. You just like what she left you. Why don't you quit and go live on it?"

"That money's to help my niece pay for her children's college, not that it's any of your mind," Fannie retorted.

Liz's senses went on alert. The countess' will had been read. It seemed a bit soon, she thought, but then she realized the countess had died last Sunday night—almost a week ago. If she could find out who else had been mentioned, she'd have a lineup of motivated suspects.

Meanwhile, she'd find out what she could. "I guess both of you were off the night the countess died," she said. "It must have been awful, the next morning, finding out what happened."

"Oh, we were here Sunday night," Fannie said. "We usually get Sundays off after breakfast, but there was a dinner party here that night so Miss Jane gave us Saturday off instead."

"We knew that night what happened," Myrtle said. "Miss Jane woke us up and told us."

So, her suppositions were right, Liz thought. There *was* a dinner party the night of the murder. She frowned. Ike must have known about it from his interviewing and hadn't mentioned it.

"Was it a big, formal dinner, like you told me about, Fannie, with the best china and all?" she asked.

"It wasn't as big as some, but it was big enough for the Theodore Roosevelt dishes," Fannie replied. "Besides Miss Jane and the family, some of Mr. Alistair's old friends from before he went to England, and Count Zanardi and Mr. Stanky."

Liz felt a throb of excitement at the mention of the two ex-husbands. Their presence in the house on the night of the murder made them suspects.

To hide her excitement, she turned to Myrtle. "What did you cook that night? I know it was something delicious."

A pleased expression spread over Myrtle's face. "Prime ribs of beef with Yorkshire pudding," she replied. "With Mr. Alistair back from England and his wife an English lady, I knew they'd like that. I made little pan roasted potatoes, too, and asparagus with me special hollandaise sauce, and chocolate cake for dessert, like I used to make when I worked for Lord and Lady Nottingham. Lord Nottingham, he was partial to my chocolate cake."

"If I wasn't filling up on this great lamb dinner, my mouth would be watering," Liz said. She directed her attention to eating for a few moments, before saying, "I hope the countess enjoyed herself, it being her last dinner, and all."

"I wouldn't know, me being down here in the kitchen," Myrtle replied. "But I heard the music after dinner and it sounded like they was all having a party."

"Well I can tell you it was a party all right and Miss Harriet had a good time," Fannie said. "There was two kinds of wine with dinner. Miss Harriet, she was tipsy before they left the table. She turned the music on loud in the parlor and was dancing wild in the front hall with all the men. She had some more drinks—and Count Zanardi and

Mr. Stanky, they had to help her up to her room. Miss Jane went with them to get her settled in bed."

Again, Liz tingled with excitement. Knowing the two ex-husbands and Miss Jane had been in the countess' bedroom the night of the murder was a big breakthrough. She pressed on.

"Sounds like the countess stayed friendly with her ex-husbands."

"Oh, she did," Fannie replied. "Especially the count. She'd never have divorced him if he wasn't such a play-boy."

"Well, it's good she enjoyed her last hours on earth. I heard on TV that her brother found her, is that right?"

"Yes," Fannie replied. "Mr. Alistair woke up when the smoke alarm outside his bedroom went off, but poor Miss Harriet, she never heard the smoke alarm at her end of the hall."

"It must have been awful for her brother, finding her like that. You knew them when they were children, Fannie. Were they close?"

Fannie shook her head. "They weren't close at all. Miss Harriet, she was very jealous of Mr. Alistair. To tell the truth, of the two of them it was plain he was his parents' favorite. I used to feel sorry for her. She didn't get half the attention Mr. Alistair did. She got back at him by being mean to him every chance she got."

More good stuff, Liz thought. It sounded as if Alistair Hunterdon had gone to England to get away from his sister.

Fannie's next words bore this out. "When their mother died Miss Harriet and Mr. Alistair came into a lot of money and that's when he took off for England. It's my guess he couldn't stand living with Miss Harriet after both his parents passed."

"I wonder why he came back?"

"When Miss Harriet got word he was coming back, I heard her telling Miss Jane she thought it was because he'd probably used up most of the money their mother left him. This house was left to him and Miss Harriet, both, and he was going to bring his family here and move in, Miss Harriet said."

Another gem to add to her trove of information, Liz thought. "He was gone a long time, wasn't he?" she asked.

"About twenty years."

"I hope they got along better after he came back."

"Not that I could see," Fannie replied. "After they moved in, Miss Harriet took it out on his wife and boys too."

With all the talk, there hadn't been any mention that the countess' death wasn't accidental. It was as if Fannie and Myrtle had closed their eyes to the fact that she'd been murdered. Come to think of it, Miss Jane hadn't mentioned it, either. She'd said only that there'd been a death here.

She decided she had enough information to start with. She finished her dinner without any more questions.

Myrtle pushed away her empty pie plate and got to her feet. "Well, I'm tired. I'm going to me room," she said. Ignoring the dishes to be cleared away, she waddled off.

"Don't cooks help with the dishes?" Liz asked Fannie.

"Not this one," Fannie replied. "In the high and mighty English homes where she worked I guess they had plenty of other maids and the cook didn't do anything but get meals. That's why she had the terrible row with Miss Harriet about helping me see to the bedrooms and baths. To tell the truth, I'm sick of her talk about her being cook for dukes and duchesses and lords and ladies and such." She paused, casting a keen glance at Liz. "I noticed she's taken a liking to you."

"That's probably because with me here, she won't have to help tend the bedrooms and baths anymore," Liz replied, with a laugh.

"Maybe," Fannie said. "But she doesn't like *me* at all. I know it's because I got fed up with her bragging and told her I didn't want to hear any more of it."

"Do you know if she came over recently? Is this her first job in the United States?"

"Miss Jane told me she's been here a few years and before she came to us she worked in a Manhattan restaurant."

Quite a comedown from cooking dinner for the Prince of Wales, Liz thought.

She went to her room, and before she started unpacking she took her new cell phone out of her purse and called Gram.

"I've been waiting for your call," Gram said. "How are things going?"

"Great," Liz replied. To make sure she wouldn't be overheard, she sat on the bed, cradled the phone in the pillow and lowered her voice. "I found out more in this one evening than I ever could have wormed out of Ike the other night. I'm sorry I can't talk long this time, Gram. I have to finish unpacking and then I expect Fannie—she's the other maid—will want to show me around. By the way, I'm a chambermaid. I guess that means I'll have to turn down the beds."

"Be sure to plump up the pillows," Gram said, "And don't forget, I'm going to take a stroll over to Moravian cemetery tomorrow afternoon. All the suspects will be at the gravesite, and there's a lot to be learned from body language. Call me tomorrow night."

Liz smiled as she said good-bye. It was clear where her interest in homicides had come from. She knew if there were anything to be picked up at Countess Zanardi's burial service, Gram would latch onto it.

Chapter Six

She'd just ended her talk with Gram when a knock
sounded on her door, followed by Fannie's voice. "Beth,
are you done unpacking? I want to take you up to the bedrooms before they get back from the funeral home."

Liz had put what little she'd brought—her clothes, slip-
pers, pajamas and underwear—in the closet and drawers.
She'd placed a framed photo of Pop and Mom and one of
Sophie on the dresser top, along with the small box where
she kept her notebook locked when she wasn't writing in
it. She didn't own a bedspread, but she'd brought along the
patchwork quilt Gram had given her for her sofa bed.

She opened the door. "I'm almost finished. I can unpack
the rest later."

Fannie peered into the room. Liz knew she couldn't miss
Gram's quilt. "You're fixing this up real nice." she said.

The remark implied the room still had a way to go, Liz
thought, but this was it. She wasn't going to pull a Martha
Stewart for only three days.

She followed Fannie down the corridor and across the
kitchen to a door. When Fannie opened the door. Liz
looked up into a steep, dark staircase.

"This here's the servants' stairs," Fannie said, switching
on an overhead light bulb.

58

When they reached the top, they stepped into a long corridor. To the right, Liz saw a broad stairway winding down to the lower floor. To the left, along the hall were several doors. She wondered which was the door to the countess' bedroom.

As if she guessed what Liz was thinking, Fannie gestured towards the other end of the hall, saying, "Miss Harriet's bedroom's down there, the last door. Nobody's been in there since the police was here."

This would have been the time for Fannie to mention something about the murder, Liz thought. Again, no M word. Though it was understandable that she might be reluctant to discuss it, it seemed strange that she hadn't said anything about it at all.

She eyed the door to the countess' room and told herself she'd have a look in there before her three days were up.

Glancing at the ceiling above where she was standing, she saw a smoke alarm. She checked out the doors. Since Alistair Hunterdon had been the first to hear the alarm, the door nearest to it must be his bedroom.

Her glance roved along the corridor ceiling and found another smoke alarm just outside the countess' bedroom. Though it might possibly be too far away for Alistair to hear, the occupants of the other bedrooms could have heard it, she thought, especially whoever was in the one closest to the countess'. She quelled her impatience to know who slept in which bedroom. She'd find out, soon enough.

"This here's the room of Mr. Alistair and his wife," Fannie said, opening the first door.

A bed with a massive, walnut headboard, and covered with a rose and cream damask spread, dominated the large room. It was flanked by matching nightstands and lamps with fringed shades. A tufted, cream-colored satin chaise heaped with rose and creamy lace pillows and draped with a white throw, stood near a bank of lace-curtained windows. A handsome Persian rug covered most of the gleaming, parquet wood floor.

Photographs in silver frames crowded lace-draped dresser tops. One photo showed Sylvia Hunterdon as a bride. In another, Alistair Hunterdon, in riding habit, posed with his horse.

More photographs lined the fireplace mantel. Their sons as babies, and during the various stages of childhood. Two older couples, probably Sylvia's parents and Alistair's. She was about to turn away when another photo caught her eye. A group picture. It was an outdoor shot. It looked like a garden wedding reception. Yes it was. There was Sylvia Hunterdon surrounded by a bevy of flower girls and several women guests wearing the typically English hats.

Examining the photo more closely, Liz stared in startled recognition. There was no mistaking the face of Queen Elizabeth beneath one of those hats. Sylvia Hunterdon must be part of the British uppercrust, she decided—a titled family. *Lady Sylvia*. And Queen Elizabeth had come to her wedding.

Fannie had already stepped over to the bed and folded back the spread. Deftly, she turned down the creamy-white top sheet over a white blanket that looked like cashmere. Remembering Gram's remark, Liz held back a laugh when she saw Fannie plump up the pillows.

Opening one of the closet doors, Fannie took out a man's dark blue bathrobe. In a house like this it would be called a dressing gown, Liz thought. From the other closet, Fannie brought out a woman's robe. Rose color. Even from across the room, Liz could tell it was pure silk. These, Fannie placed on either side at the foot of the bed.

After a brief inspection of the bathroom, Fannie gave a nod. "Now we'll go to Miss Jane's room."

That meant the boys were in the rooms closest to the countess', Liz thought. Surely one of them would have been awakened by the first alarm. But maybe not. Kids slept soundly.

Miss Jane's room wasn't as richly furnished as the first.

Everything, from the green and tan brocade bedspread to the green broadloom carpet looked a little worn. Still, the room gave out a pleasant aura of comfort. An armchair drawn up to the fireplace. Books everywhere. But no photographs. That was odd, Liz thought.

"Doesn't Miss Jane have any family?" she asked Fannie.

Fannie shook her head. "No, she was alone in the world after her husband died."

"You'd think she'd have a picture of her late husband."

Fannie's reply was almost explosive. "Miss Harriet told me he was a no-good, drunken bum who abused her and said he'd kill her if she left him. Miss Jane was a nurse and he spent all her hard-earned money on liquor. His passing was a blessing for her." She paused. "You might as well know it as not—he didn't just die. Someone shot him dead outside a bar."

Startled, Liz asked, "Did the police get whoever did it?"

"Witnesses said the husband had words with some guy in the bar, but he was never found. Poor Miss Jane, she was in such a shock, she couldn't work. And she had no money. That's why Miss Harriet took her in."

That was a true act of kindness, Liz thought. But something Ike had said came back to puzzle her. Miss Jane didn't appear to be grieving over the countess' death, he'd told her. Why wouldn't losing her friend and benefactor have devastated her?

"You want to turn down Miss Jane's bed while I get her robe out?" Fannie asked.

Liz tucked this last thought into a corner of her mind. She'd get back to it when she wasn't so distracted. "Sure," she said.

She folded back the slightly shabby spread and brought the plain white sheet in a neat triangle down over the light green blanket. She plumped up the pillows, again thinking of Gram and smiling to herself.

Fannie draped a pink-and-white-checked cotton robe

over the foot of the bed. After casting a quick glance into the bathroom, she turned and headed for the door. "The boys' rooms next and then we're done," she said.

They entered the first room. Fannie said it was Mr. David's. Liz noticed the furnishings were much nicer than Miss Jane's. A new looking, dark blue bedspread. A blue and rose Oriental rug. Two comfortable-looking armchairs. Nice lamps. A handsome walnut desk. Overflowing bookshelves. She checked out some of the book titles. *Dr. Jekyl and Mr. Hyde. The Hound of the Baskervilles. The Valley of Fear.* Apparently David was a serious kid, into classical reading, and he liked books with a macabre twist.

"You turn down the bed and I'll tidy up the bathroom," Fannie said.

After tending to the bed, Liz found a tartan plaid robe in the closet and brought it out. Fannie was still straightening up the bathroom. *"Boys,"* Liz heard her mutter.

She followed Fannie through the bathroom into the elder son's room, also handsomely furnished. But unlike David's room, posters of luxury cars hung along one wall—a Rolls Royce, a Mercedes, a Porsche and a BMW. She wasn't surprised to see posters of bikini-clad girls on another section of wall. She recalled being stared at by this kid at the dinner table. She suspected he'd been visualizing her in an abbreviated swimsuit, or even less.

David Hunterdon's room was separated from his brother's by their bathroom. She did some calculating. The bathroom and bedrooms were large. The bathroom plus Randolph's room would put maybe twenty feet between David's room and the smoke alarm outside the countess' door. He might not have heard it. But the alarm was fairly close to Randolph's door. It seemed as if even a sound sleeper would have heard it and responded in time to save the countess.

But Randolph didn't strike her as a killer. A girl-crazy teenager, sure, but not vicious. Besides, what possible motive would he have for wanting his aunt dead? He'd only lived here for a week or so.

With all the beds turned down and robes laid out, Fannie led the way down the hall and onto the back stairway. "They won't be needing you anymore tonight," she told Liz, as they descended to the kitchen. "Mornings we get up at seven. Me and Myrtle, we see to breakfast and while they're in the dining room that's when you do the bedrooms. I don't serve at breakfast. I put everything on the sideboard and they help themselves."

"I hope I do everything right," Liz said. "Miss Jane told me the sheets are changed tomorrow and towels get changed every day. How do I know who gets which sheets and towels?"

"Sheets for all the beds except Miss Jane's have a fancy H embroidered on them," Fannie replied. "All the towels are white and very fluffy and marked with the H except Miss Jane's. All the linens are in the hall closet. Cleaning supplies are in each bathroom cabinet. Throw what needs to be washed down the chute in the linen closet. It goes down to the laundry room. But don't worry. I'll be up to help you before you're even half done."

In the kitchen, she told Liz to finish her unpacking. "Then go to bed if you feel like it. I have to wait and see if they want anything when they get back." She smiled, flashing a gold tooth. "You caught onto everything quick, Beth. I hope you'll stay with us a long time. No reason not to, now."

In her room, Liz finished unpacking. She set her portable radio on the dresser. She missed her TV already, but the radio would keep her up to date on the investigation of Countess Zanardi's murder.

She was undressed when she decided to take a shower. Poking her head out the door, she looked down the hall and saw that the door to the bathroom was open. She put her robe on, grabbed her toilet articles and headed towards it. On the way she passed a room with a partially open door and glimpsed Fannie watching TV. Across the hall was a room with a closed door. This had to be Myrtle's room, she decided.

On an impulse, she knocked on the door, saying, "Myrtle, it's me, Beth. I'm going to take a shower and I thought maybe you might like to use the bathroom first."

Myrtle opened the door. She looked enormous in a black rayon robe with pink and red blossoms strewn from shoulder to hem. Her pudgy face bore its most pleasant expression yet. "Well, if I do say so meself, that's very thoughtful, Beth. Nothing I hate more than having to go and Fannie in there taking her own sweet time. But I already been, so you have your bath."

More brownie points with Myrtle, Liz thought. Tomorrow, she'd drop a few discreet questions when Fannie wasn't around. Maybe Myrtle would be more forthright than Fannie. Maybe she'd mention the countess' death was a murder. And, although Myrtle wasn't in as close touch with the other occupants of the house as Fannie, she could have noticed or heard something.

After showering, she settled herself in bed, turned on the lamp and started to write in her notebook. For every homicide case she followed, she kept a record of possible suspects and clues, and the investigation's progress. She was off to a good start on this one.

If the motive was money, and it looked as if it might be, she already had five possible suspects—Alistair Hunterdon, Miss Jane, Fannie and the two ex-husbands. If she wanted to stretch it, she could add Randolph to the list. His proximity to the smoke alarm outside the countess' bedroom would be damning if she could figure out how the death of his aunt would benefit him.

Ike would know, she thought. By this time he'd checked every beneficiary in the will. With a sigh, she put down her pen and closed her notebook. Following a homicide wasn't as much fun without Ike's input. She'd grown accustomed to trading ideas with him about motives and suspects. She missed this. She missed Ike.

She turned her radio on to a news station. If the police had released some new information about the case to the media, maybe she could piece it together with what she'd found out for herself.

Coverage of the case was nothing but a rehash. Did that mean Ike and his partner hadn't come up with anything since they were assigned to the case? No, she decided. In the three days since the countess' death was declared a homicide, they'd have found *something*. They just weren't ready to release it to the media, just as they hadn't released the report about the coma-causing substance in the countess' booze bottle, and the fact that the incriminating bottle hadn't been found.

At that moment she'd have given anything to be back in her apartment, tossing possible clues around with Ike, and getting information the news media didn't know yet.

She tried to bolster her sagging spirits by reminding herself that she'd find out a lot tomorrow. After the funeral, the house would be thronged with people who'd known the countess and Alistair for years, including the two ex-husbands. She'd be helping Fannie in the dining room. If she kept her eyes and ears open, there was no telling what she'd pick up.

Chapter Seven

T he next morning Liz put on the black uniform and plain
white apron.

In the kitchen, Fannie was at the table, drinking coffee.
Myrtle, at the stove, had just poured herself a mug of tea
and was spooning sugar into it. Four heaping spoonfuls,
Liz noticed.

Fannie nodded approval when she saw Liz. "I meant to
tell you last night, wear the black for working upstairs and
change to the gray with the fancy apron for after the funeral."

"Sit down, Ducky. Have some breakfast," Myrtle said.
She brought a mug down from the dish cabinet. "Do you
take coffee or tea?"

*Ducky! And is Myrtle actually going to fill the mug and
bring it to me?*

"Coffee, please," she managed to say.

"Here you are," Myrtle said, putting the coffee mug on
the table. "Sugar and milk's right there. I have scones in
the oven. They'll be ready in a twink. I'm going to make
eggs and ham for the dining room. I could fix some for
you now, if you'd like."

Almost overwhelmed, Liz told Myrtle she'd settle for a
scone. Gram knew what she was talking about when she

said you could catch more flies with honey than with vinegar.

"You better get going on the ham and eggs, Myrtle," Fannie said. "You know I need to put everything out before they come down. And be sure you make enough. Yesterday Mr. Randolph went back for seconds and there wasn't hardly anything left."

Myrtle's only response was a cold glare, as she opened the oven and withdrew a pan.

Liz hadn't tasted anything quite like the scone Myrtle put on a plate and placed in front of her. Hearty, yet light and just sweet enough. She should ask Myrtle for her recipe, she thought. This would be something Ike would enjoy with coffee while they were watching a late movie. She thrust away the thought. No scones for Ike till he shaped up in the information department.

She helped Fannie load the dumbwaiter with a pitcher of orange juice, covered platters of scrambled eggs and ham, a silver filigree basket of scones, plates of butter, dishes of jam, china tea and coffeepots and cream pitcher and sugar bowl. They hoisted it all up to the serving pantry. Then Fannie went up to arrange everything on the sideboard.

Alone with Myrtle, Liz seized the chance to have a few words with her before going to tend the bedrooms. There wasn't time to ease into the subject slowly. "Myrtle," she said, "I know you haven't worked here long, but you must have some ideas about the circumstances of the countess' death."

Myrtle stared at her. "About the police saying someone done her in? Nobody around here believes that. Not Miss Jane or none of the others. Not the count or Mr. Stanky neither."

So this was why nothing had been said about murder, Liz thought. It wasn't hard to understand why anyone who knew the countess would reject the idea of homicide. Apparently they all knew she habitually went to bed inebriated and that she always had a drink of vodka after hitting the sack. They also knew her efforts to quit smoking hadn't succeeded. It made sense that she'd fallen into a drunken stupor with a lit cigarette in her hand, and dropped it onto the carpet.

She pieced together what she knew with what Ike might know but hadn't told her. Only the killer knew the countess was in a coma from drinking contaminated booze *before* she died of smoke inhalation. By withholding this information, the police could have made the killer believe that the autopsy hadn't picked up the toxic substance. Dan said it was called isopropanol and it was close to ethyl alcohol. Maybe the murderer decided it hadn't been found during autopsy because of the large amount of alcohol already consumed by the countess.

It looked as if the killer had been led to believe the ruling of homicide was based solely on the autopsy results—no cigarette smoke in the countess' system. And it was the killer who started household members believing the autopsy was botched.

Smoke. This entire case revolved around it.

This was Ike's strategy, she decided. He was using the smoke to cover up the coma-inducing substance found at autopsy. He was counting on the smoke cover giving the killer a false sense of security. If the presence of the toxic substance in the countess' system remained under cover, the killer might get careless.

Assuming the murderer was a member of the household or one of the two ex-husbands, she knew she must keep her eyes and ears open during the post-funeral feast. The perpetrator's overconfidence might lead to self-betrayal.

Her thoughts returned to Myrtle, who must be waiting for a response to her last statement. "But the autopsy showed the countess hadn't been smoking . . ."

Myrtle gave a loud snort. "With all that other smoke inside her, they could have made a mistake. Everyone around here knows she was sneaking cigarettes."

Dan would get a laugh out of Myrtle's postmortem judgment, Liz thought. "So you really believe the countess passed out while smoking in bed, and dropped the cigarette?" she asked.

Myrtle nodded. "It's not only me and Miss Jane and Fannie believes that. Mr. Alistair and Lady Sylvia and the young gentlemen think so, too, and the count and Mr. Stanky."

Lady Sylvia. Liz's thoughts were temporarily diverted. So it was true—Alistair Hunterdon's wife came from British nobility. "Is Lady Sylvia as nice as she is pretty?" she asked.

Myrtle's triple chin bobbed as she nodded her head. "Pretty, and a true lady. Her coming to live here was a sign she was meant to be lady of this house. Born to her title, she was. Not like some."

A transparent dig at Harriet Hunterdon's title, acquired by marriage, Liz thought. "You didn't like the countess, did you?" she asked.

"Not me or nobody else around here." Myrtle replied. "I wasn't here a day but what I got wise to that."

Liz continued fishing. "Surely Miss Jane liked her. Weren't they close friends? Fannie told me the countess took her in—gave her a home after her husband was killed and she was down and out."

Myrtle's chins swayed to and fro as she shook her head. "No friend would talk to Miss Jane like she did. Terrible, it was—insulting. If you ask me, the countess had something on Miss Jane, or why would she put up with it?"

Much as she wanted to continue this talk, Liz knew it was time to go upstairs and tend the bedrooms. She headed for the back stairs, saying, "Maybe Miss Jane thought the countess acted mean because she was unhappy. She put up with it because she felt sorry for her."

"Maybe," Myrtle said. "Miss Jane's nice like that. Things around here are fine, now that she's in charge."

Liz paused at the foot of the back stairs. "Are you saying she's going to stay on?"

"Yes. Lady Sylvia asked her to. She and Mr. Alistair, both."

Liz's mind whirled as she climbed the stairs. Among all the bits of information, two stood out. First, everyone in the household was in denial about the murder. Second, Myrtle thought Miss Jane hadn't left because the countess had something on her. That was another way of saying *blackmail*. Later, when she wrote it all down in her notebook, she'd give this some more thought.

Stepping into the bedroom corridor, she heard voices and retreating footsteps from the direction of the front stairway. Everyone going to breakfast, she decided. She glanced down the hall and decided to start with Randolph's room. But, before she went in there, she'd have time for a quick peek into the countess' bedroom. Fannie wouldn't be up here for another few minutes. There was no need for her to go into the room. She only wanted to get a clear picture of the crime scene in her head.

When she opened the door, she almost collided with Randolph Hunterdon, wearing a dark suit, and smelling of after-shave. She knew she must look surprised, but she needn't explain why she was there. For all he knew, Miss Jane had told her to clean the countess' bathroom. It was he who should explain what he was doing in the closed-off room where his aunt had died.

"Oh, sorry," he said. "I hope I didn't startle you. My brother was monopolizing our bath, so I used this one." With that, he brushed past her and hurried down the hall towards the front stairway.

His explanation was too spontaneous not to be true, Liz thought. She'd noticed he'd been in a big hurry to get down to breakfast and he hadn't stared at her as he had last night in the dining room.

She stood in the doorway, letting her eyes take in the entire room, noticing the cigarette burn on the carpet near the bed and the charred area where the burned chair must have stood. The handsome, paisley-patterned, red damask spread had to be the same one which had been on the bed when the countess died. Both it and the array of tasseled pillows strewn on it matched the window draperies. Evidently the fire, more fumes than flame according to news reports, had been confined to the carpet and chair. Though the chair had been removed, the lingering smell of smoke and chemicals almost made her gag.

Next to the bed stood a nightstand with a small drawer and a cabinet below. The countess probably kept her booze bottle in that cabinet, Liz decided. She pictured the countess, very drunk, taking one last swig from the bottle and, a few minutes later, going into a coma.

She didn't want Fannie to catch her here, so she gave a final look and then withdrew. She found the linen closet and took out clean sheets and towels. Recalling what Fannie said, she knew which towels were Miss Jane's. They were the only ones not luxuriously thick, nor were they monogrammed. They were like the servants' towels.

Randolph's door was only a few steps away. This kid wouldn't take any prizes for neatness, Liz thought, eyeing the pajamas, socks, and other clothing on the floor. She'd just finished changing the bed when Fannie came in. Together, they tackled the boys' bathroom. By the time they finished, Liz decided when she had kids, she'd prefer all girls.

In contrast to David's and Randolph's quarters, Miss Jane's room and bath looked neat and clean. "Miss Jane's never any trouble," Fannie said, unfolding Miss Jane's sheets. As Liz noticed yesterday, they were not smooth and silky, like the bedding for the family bedrooms.

Again, she saw how seedy Miss Jane's room looked, compared to all the others. It was as if the countess had all the bedrooms except Miss Jane's redecorated regularly. This, plus the verbal abuse Myrtle described; yet Miss Jane continued to live here and put up with it. Why? Liz had to admit Myrtle's supposition might not be far off mark. The countess might have been holding something over Miss Jane's head. She'd think about that some more when she wrote about it in her notebook.

Fannie's voice came into her thoughts. "Now for Mr. Alistair's bedroom and then we're done up here."

Entering the last bedroom, the photo of Queen Elizabeth reminded Liz of what Myrtle had said about Mrs. Alistair Hunterdon. "Myrtle told me Mr. Alistair's wife comes from a titled family," she said. "I guess that means I should address her as Lady Sylvia."

Fannie's reply was half-grunt, half-laugh. "Myrtle's hipped on titles," she said, as they started replacing the bed's silky-smooth sheets with a fresh set. "You call her whatever you want. Me, I'll stick to ma'am." She paused, unfurling a monogrammed top sheet. "Don't get me wrong. I got nothing against Mr. Alistair's wife, but I'm not going to kowtow to her like she's any better than us plain Americans."

Liz suppressed a smile. Myrtle might be overly impressed by titles, but Fannie certainly wasn't. However, from Myrtle's standpoint, Countess Harriet Hunterdon Zanardi was only second rate when compared to Lady Sylvia Hunterdon. To get Fannie's reaction, she said, "Myrtle must have loved being in the same house with two titled women."

Fannie nodded. "At first she was tickled pink, but she soon changed her mind about Miss Harriet. Like I told you before, when Miss Harriet told Myrtle she had to help with the bedrooms, she got huffy and they had words. If it hadn't been for Miss Jane, she'd have quit on the spot."

"Sounds like Miss Jane is sort of a peacemaker around here," Liz said.

Fannie's eyes softened. "She's the real royal one around here."

Liz wanted to mention that Myrtle thought the countess had been holding something over Miss Jane's head. That could wait, she decided. First, she'd get Fannie's input on the cause of the countess' death.

"Myrtle told me nobody around here believes that someone set the fire. You're all sure the countess' death was an accident," she said.

"That's right, an accident," Fannie replied. "It's a miracle it didn't happen sooner, with her drinking and smoking in bed."

"Then you don't believe she'd given up smoking?"

"We all knew the doctor told her to quit, but sometimes when I made her bed, I could smell cigarette smoke. I never found any butts, though. I guess she flushed them down the toilet the next morning. When I told Miss Jane, she said she wasn't surprised. She knew Miss Harriet was sneaking smokes."

"But the police said no nicotine showed up during the autopsy."

"There was so much other smoke in her, how could they know, for sure?" Fannie said. "They could have made a mistake. Myrtle told us about a case in England where the police said someone set a fire that killed a woman, but her family wouldn't believe it, and in the end it turned out to be an accident, after all. The same thing could happen with Miss Harriet. Miss Jane told us that Mr. Alistair's going to talk to the district attorney about it."

This sounded as if Alistair Hunterdon might be taking steps to have the homicide ruling reversed, Liz thought.

"Well, we're all done up here," Fannie said. "We should see how things are in the dining room. They should be near done by now."

She led the way down the back stairs into the kitchen, then up the flight to the serving pantry. Looking into the dining room, Liz didn't think anyone showed any signs of finishing. Randolph and David were at the sideboard, re-filling their plates. The others were drinking coffee and talking among themselves.

"We'll have lunch at twelve," Liz heard Miss Jane say.

"I thought we'd be too crowded in the BMW so I ordered a limousine. It will be here at one o'clock."

David returned to the table, asking, "How long will the service be?"

"It should be over by three," Alistair Hunterdon replied.

"How long does it take to get to the cemetery?" Randolph asked.

"About an hour and a half," Miss Jane said.

Randolph's voice took on a whine. "And at least a half hour for the graveside service and another hour and a half returning. Why couldn't the service have been earlier? We'll miss tea. I'll be starved by the time we get back here."

"Now, Randy darling, you mustn't complain," Lady Sylvia chided. Her voice sounded like dialogue in a British movie, Liz thought.

"We'll eat as soon as we get back, Randy," Miss Jane added. "We have a refrigerator full of all kinds of wonderful food people sent over. The maids will have everything ready. We expect there'll be a big crowd here, but you and David can dive right in."

"With that big crowd, let's hope there's enough to go round," Randolph growled.

For a nineteen-year-old, Randolph Hunterdon acted like a spoiled brat, Liz thought. Of the two brothers, David, the younger one, seemed the more mature.

When everyone left the table, she and Fannie started the usual routine of clearing, loading the dumbwaiter and sending it down to the kitchen. After they'd finished transferring the dishes into the dishwasher, Liz hoped she'd have some time to herself. She wanted to get to her notebook while her observations were still fresh in her mind.

Her hopes faded when Fannie told her Miss Jane wanted them to do some cleaning before lunch. "With all the people coming, she wants the downstairs dusted and vacuumed."

"How many rooms?" Liz asked.

"Dining room, parlor and library, that's three, and the reception hall makes four," Fannie replied. "And there's the downstairs lavatory, but that won't need more than a quick wipe."

If the Hunterdon brothers had been in the downstairs lavatory, it would need more than that, Liz thought.

"What do we do if someone's sitting around in one of the rooms?" she asked. She couldn't quite picture herself asking Alistair Hunterdon to raise his feet while she vacuumed around his chair.

"If that happens, you just skip that room and go back later. But most of the time if someone's there they tell you to go ahead with your work, they were just leaving anyway."

As it turned out, nobody was in any of the rooms. Liz decided they were all upstairs, messing up their nice, clean bedrooms and baths.

Except for the dining room, she hadn't seen the downstairs rooms before. The marble-floored reception hall with the broad, graceful stairway was almost bare of furnishing. Two enormous vases which might have come from some Ming dynasty palace, flanked the entrance. It looked like a ballroom, Liz thought. She pictured a nineteenth century ball in progress. Pompadoured ladies in swoon-inducing gowns waltzing with gentlemen in tailcoats and white ties and stiffly starched white shirts.

In the parlor, she admired the tasteful opulence of antique mahogany, a concert grand piano, quietly elegant upholstery, oil paintings in gold leaf frames, delicate bibelots in a gilded cabinet, and beneath it all, a rug which could have graced the Taj Mahal.

In the library, shelves of richly bound books on ceiling-high walnut shelves lined most of the walls. Reading lamps and buttery-soft leather chairs clustered around a huge walnut table. A leather sofa stood near a marble fireplace where an oil painting of a nineteenth century woman hung above the mantel.

Dusting and vacuuming amid all this splendor made Liz feel as if she were her Irish immigrant great-grandmother.

After the last room was in order, Fannie said they could take a break. "Miss Jane expects us to stop for some rest before it's time to serve lunch," she said. "Miss Jane's no slave driver."

Good, Liz thought. At last she could get to her notebook. In the kitchen, they found Myrtle at the stove, stirring the savory-smelling contents of a large pot. "Vegetable barley soup with what's left of yesterday's lamb," she announced. "They'll need something hearty to carry them through the funeral and all. I'll make potato salad too. With the soup and some biscuits, and cake for dessert, that should do." She paused, tossing her head, sending her chins into action. "I used to make lamb and vegetable barley soup when I was cook for the Duke and Duchess of Talkington," she said. "Wild about me soup, the duke was."

After three days of Myrtle's cooking, going back to her microwaved dinners wouldn't be easy. Liz thought.

In her room, she curled up on the bed with her pen and notebook, ready to record what she'd found out since she'd assumed the role of Beth the chambermaid.

Chapter Eight

She'd just opened her notebook when she heard loud talk coming from the kitchen. Myrtle's voice, then Fannie's, but she couldn't make out what they were saying. It wouldn't surprise her if they were having an argument. Myrtle's bragging rubbed Fannie the wrong way.

But sometimes revealing statements were made during the heat of an argument, she thought. Maybe she could pick up something. She put her notebook in the box, locked it and stashed it in a dresser drawer before opening the door and stepping out into the corridor.

Myrtle's voice, loud and angry, floated down the hall. "If you ask me, he's got some cheek coming here the day of the funeral."

Fannie's voice sounded angry, too, but more subdued. "Poor Miss Jane, she was very upset when I told her he was here again."

"He didn't ask to see anyone else?" Myrtle asked.

"No, only Miss Jane. I showed him into the parlor. Miss Jane said she'd see him out when they were done talking."

"As if the police hadn't done enough harm, calling the countess' death a murder," Myrtle said. "And now they're hounding Miss Jane, like they think . . ."

Liz had heard enough. She darted back into her room,

closed the door and took a deep breath. But she couldn't shut out the startling realization that Ike was here, in the house. If he'd arrived a few minutes ago, they might have come face to face in the reception hall.

Gram was right. She shouldn't have counted on Ike not coming back for further interviewing. But why only Miss Jane? She took her notebook out of the box and wrote this question down, along with other questions concerning Miss Jane.

Was Miss Jane Ike's prime suspect?

Why had she continued to live here when the countess treated her with such disrespect?

Was Myrtle right? Had the countess been holding something over her head?

If she could pin down a motive for the murder, she might come up with some answers. Thus far, she had only the assumption that the killer was a beneficiary of the countess' will. Was Miss Jane one of the lucky ones? Was that why Ike had come to question her again? But, after treating her like dirt for nine years, why would the countess leave her anything?

A knock sounded on her door, followed by Fannie's voice. "Change into your serving uniform, Beth. It's almost time for lunch."

Liz sighed. That meant the usual hassle of loading everything onto the dumbwaiter, hoisting it up to the serving pantry and waiting on a dining room table full of people who hadn't a clue how the other half lived. With the exception of Miss Jane, she thought, remembering the no-good husband.

No sooner was the lunch routine over and the family gone to the funeral service, when Fannie said she must do some laundry.

"I'm never caught up," she said. "There's still things from yesterday in the dryer, and now there's the sheets and towels to wash from this morning."

"Miss Jane told me I'd be expected to help you," Liz said.

Fannie nodded. "You could take the stuff out of the dryer, while I'm loading up the washer again," she said, as they headed for the laundry room.

Myrtle, drinking a mug of tea at the kitchen table, said, "While you're at it, you can do up a few of me duds."

Fannie looked as if she were about to make a sharp retort. Instead, she gave a curt nod. "Bring them to the laundry room," she said.

In the laundry room, she turned to Liz with an exasperated sigh. "I told Miss Jane I shouldn't be expected to wash Myrtle's dirty clothes. Myrtle treats me like she's one of those English duchesses she worked for, and I'm her servant. Miss Jane agreed with me, but she asked me would I do it to keep peace."

Fannie would do anything for Miss Jane, Liz decided.

Fannie got a washer load going and Liz emptied the dryer. After they'd finished folding a batch of towels and put them in a basket to be taken upstairs, Fannie told Liz they needed to polish all the silverware. "I know it looks okay, but with company coming today, Miss Jane wants everything shined up extra good."

By the time they'd polished what seemed like hundreds of sterling silver knives, forks and spoons, several Paul Revere-style bowls, tea and coffeepots and trays, Liz felt bone weary. She had a small pain in her back and her feet hurt.

Myrtle, who'd been watching them polish the silver while she snacked on a wedge of leftover pie, cast Liz an understanding look. "You're not used to this much work, are you, Ducks?"

"My last place was with just one old lady, and her house was nothing like this one," Liz replied.

Before Myrtle could beat Fannie to it in what seemed to be developing into a good-maid-bad-maid competition,

Fannie said, "You go take a nice hot shower, Beth, and then rest a while."

Liz's rest turned into a nap. When she wakened it was after 4 o'clock.

A few minutes later Fannie knocked on her door. She opened it with a smile. "Looks like you had a good rest," Fannie said.

"I fell asleep," Liz replied. "I guess it's time for us to set up the dining room. I'll be ready in a couple of minutes." Then she remembered the routine of turning down the beds. "Oh, instead of sleeping I should have attended to the bedrooms early so I could get down to the dining room and help you. I'll hurry through the bedrooms, now."

"Don't worry, I already did them," Fannie said. She gave a wry smile. "Myrtle said not to wake Ducky up."

While getting into her uniform, Liz remembered that Gram would be strolling around Moravian cemetery about now, keeping her eyes peeled. "You can learn a lot from body language," she'd said. If there should be any interaction among those at Harriet Hunterdon Zanardi's graveside, or any unusual activity, Gram would be sure to pick up on it.

She didn't know if anything Gram picked up might shed light on the countess' murder, but sometimes a seemingly irrelevant bit of information could lead to an important clue. She'd helped Ike solve his last two cases that way. Despite his reluctance to tell her anything about this case, she still wanted to come up with something to help him. Wasn't that one reason why she was here?

But, lurking in the back of her mind was the troublesome thought that she'd have to tell him she'd gone undercover at the Hunterdon house instead of spending the weekend with Gram. She'd have to confess she'd lied to him. Would things ever be the same between them after that?

By 6:30 she and Fannie had the dining room table laden with platters of roast beef, ham, and chicken, and a variety of casserole dishes, salads, relishes and sandwiches. Cooks in the kitchens of the Hunterdon's high-society friends had been busy, following a tradition which transcended social levels.

One end of the massive mahogany sideboard was set up with coffee and tea services. Nearby stood a variety of wines and liquors, mixers, silver ice buckets and appropriate glasses. Layer cakes, petit fours, fancy cookies, bon-bons, nuts and mints were arranged at the opposite end.

They'd placed groups of chairs around the room and set up a number of small tables. "The tables are for them that don't like eating off their laps," Fannie explained. "Folks will mostly serve themselves. We help anyone who needs it, and watch to make sure there's enough of everything."

By 7 o'clock the huge dining room was crowded. Most were fiftyish couples, Liz noticed, with a sprinkling of elderly people.

"The countess had a lot of friends," she whispered to Fannie.

"They're mostly Mr. Alistair's friends, and the older people, they're friends of Miss Harriet's and Mr. Alistair's parents," Fannie said. "But see that big man getting wine? The one with the graying hair? He's Miss Harriet's first husband."

Gus Stanky's baggy tweed jacket and khakis stood out in this assembly of dark, custom-made suits. Even with gray hair and a slight paunch, he still looked like a linebacker, Liz thought. It wasn't hard to picture him as the young, handsome hunk who'd swept the Madcap Deb off her feet. She was wondering why they'd divorced, when Miss Jane joined him. He poured her a glass of wine. Something about the way they looked at each other sent Liz an intuitive message. Those two liked each other. It might even go beyond liking, she decided, watching them walk away into the crowd.

"Miss Jane and Mr. Stanky look like they're friends," she said to Fannie.

"They are," Fannie replied.

They spoke in near whispers, even though the hum of conversation in the room would have made what they said inaudible.

"Mr. Stanky, he's a good man," Fannie said. "He and Miss Harriet were divorced a long time when Miss Jane came here, but like the other one, he still came around a lot." She glanced over her shoulder to make sure nobody was nearby before continuing. "Miss Jane found out he was in trouble from betting on racehorses. If he hadn't stopped his betting, he would have lost the farm he got with the divorce money. Miss Jane helped him quit."

"He's stopped gambling?"

Fannie nodded. "Miss Jane got him going to meetings— the kind like heavy drinkers go to when they want to stop drinking."

Another indication of Miss Jane's good heart, and an interesting slant on husband number one, Liz thought. "Is the second husband here?" she asked.

"He's over there near the window, talking to Mr. Alistair's wife," Fannie said.

The cliché, tall, dark and handsome, fit playboy Count Paolo Zanardi perfectly, Liz thought. She noticed he was standing a little too close to Lady Sylvia, and the way he was whispering in her ear, suggested he was hitting on her. Lady Sylvia, conservatively chic in black with pearls, seemed to be taking it with the traditional British stiff upper lip.

At the other end of the table, she saw Alistair Hunterdon talking to a distinguished-looking black gentleman. The conversation seemed to be serious. Instinct told her she might find their talk interesting. Just as she was wondering how she could eavesdrop on them, she noticed an elderly lady near them having difficulty spearing a slice of roast beef onto her plate.

In an instant, Liz was at her side, helping her. She was

close enough to Alistair and the other gentleman to hear every word they spoke.

"Do you think I might have a case, counselor?" Alistair asked.

So the black gentleman was an attorney. Liz took her time with the elderly lady's plate and kept her ears perked.

"From what you've told me, there could be a chance," the attorney replied. "I don't know of any precedent, but I'll do some research."

Still talking, the two men moved away from the table. But Liz had heard enough to know that her previous supposition was true. Alistair Hunterdon was taking steps to reverse the declaration of his sister's death as a homicide. Did he consider a murder in the family a blot on the Hunterdon escutcheon, or was there another reason?

Whatever the reason, Alistair would be in for a disappointment when police released the information that someone had slipped a coma-inducing substance into her booze. That would cast doubt on his claim that she *had* been smoking that night and caused the fire herself.

She remembered her idea about Ike holding back that information—using it as a cover to help snare the killer. Would the police continue to withhold the full autopsy report until the murderer got careless and said or did something incriminating? Maybe, when she saw Ike again, he'd give her some answers. *Unless he walks out of my life after I confess I lied to him.*

She'd just stepped away from the table to stand by the sideboard near the cakes and other sweets, when she was jolted out of her thoughts by the feel of a hand on her waist. Not just on it, but *fondling* it. She whirled around and came face to face with Randolph Hunterdon.

"I've always been attracted to red-haired women," he said. He was holding a highball glass in his free hand. His speech was slurred and his rosy cheeks were even rosier.

It hadn't taken him long to get into the booze, she

thought. He hadn't learned how to handle his liquor yet. Or women, either, judging from his clumsy approach.

She tried to wriggle away. "Oh, excuse me, Mr. Randolph," she said, pretending she thought she'd bumped into him.

He ignored both her attempt to break away and her apology. "You're the only person my age in this collection of old bones," he said. "I don't mean just at this dreary affair, I mean here in this house. The minute I saw you I knew we could have some jolly good times together when you're off."

She'd dealt with passes before, but never with a male so much younger. She'd always looked younger than her years and rather enjoyed it. However, there was nothing enjoyable about being pawed by this English adolescent. While she tried to think of a remark that wouldn't wound his tender psyche, he tightened his hand on her.

"My father told me there are lovely beaches within a two-hour drive of the city," he said. "We could motor out to the seashore, spend the day, go for a swim, have tea, and . . ."

She longed to tell him to take his hand off her and get lost. Instead, not wanting to risk a scene, she said, "I couldn't do that, Mr. Randolph."

"Oh, we wouldn't let anyone know, of course," he went on, giving her waist another squeeze. "I'd have to pick you up someplace away from the house."

She felt her temper rising. This arrogant kid was a throwback to the days when wealthy young gentlemen considered servant girls fair game. She quelled the urge to reach for a chocolate cake with gooey icing and push it in his face. "A trip to the beach wouldn't be possible, Mr. Randolph," she said.

"Are you wondering how we'd get to the seashore from here?" he asked. "Don't worry your pretty redhead about that. Father says I'm to have my aunt's BMW."

Whether it was her temper ready to explode or her reaction to his statement about the BMW, she managed to wrest free of his grasp and walk away and join Fannie on the other side of the table.

Her mind teemed with speculations. Alistair and his sister had inherited their parents' estate jointly. After the countess' death, the bulk of the estate reverted to Alistair. He must have known the estate included the BMW. *When had he promised it to Randolph?*

If the promise had been made before the countess' death, would this have motivated Randolph to kill her? She shook her head. The BMW must have more than a few years on it. He wouldn't commit murder to get possession of an old car. On second thought, many young men had an intense interest in vintage luxury cars. She'd give this more thought later, when she had time to sort everything out.

Fannie was busy filling an elderly gentleman's plate. Evidently she hadn't noticed the encounter with Randolph. And it wasn't likely anyone else had, Liz decided. There'd been nothing to attract attention. She cast a furtive look around. Randolph had disappeared into the crowd.

"Beth, we're running low on coffee," Fannie said, spooning lobster thermidor onto the gentleman's plate. "Would you call the kitchen and have Myrtle send up another pot?"

When Liz called from the serving pantry, Myrtle said, "Sure, Ducky, I'll have it on in a twink. Is there enough food up there?"

Liz glanced into the dining room. "It's beginning to go, especially the roast beef," she replied.

"I'll send up extras with the coffee," Myrtle said. "That's the way it is when there's been a burying. People eat like they think they'll never eat again. When I was in service to the Duke and Duchess of Talkington one of their relatives died. I thought I'd have to move me bed into the kitchen."

Myrtle never missed a chance to hark back to her glory days, Liz thought.

The post-funeral feast continued without further incidents. When guests began leaving, Liz realized she hadn't picked up as much information as she'd hoped to. But at least she'd observed the two ex-husbands and noticed that the linebacker had something going with Miss Jane, and the count would like to get something going with Lady Sylvia.

She'd also found out that Alistair Hunterdon had sought legal advice in the matter of changing the cause of his sister's death from homicide to accidental. But the most exciting bit of information she'd picked up was Randolph's statement about the BMW.

It was almost 10 o'clock by the time she and Fannie cleared the dining room and kitchen. She'd just come in from putting the trash in the outside can when Miss Jane appeared.

"Fannie . . . Beth . . . on behalf of the family and myself, thank you," she said. "I know it was a long, tiring day, but you did a superb job. I want you to know I appreciate it."

It was no wonder Fannie adored her, Liz thought. She'd become fond of Miss Jane too. When Monday rolled around, it wouldn't be easy to tell her she was quitting. Another thought struck her. She should tell Miss Jane, tomorrow, instead of Monday. It wasn't much notice, but it was better than none. She hated to leave her in the lurch, but there was a bright spot. The countess' reputation as a mean employer was no longer a hiring handicap. Word that Miss Jane was now in charge must have spread by this time. Miss Jane wouldn't have any trouble finding a replacement.

In her room, before she got ready for bed, she phoned Gram.

"I'm sorry I'm calling so late. How did it go at the cemetery today?" she asked.

"It went fine," Gram replied. "I didn't have any trouble finding the right place. All those fancy cars. I sat on a bench in a nearby plot where I could get a good view."

"Did you see anything interesting?"

"Nothing especially interesting, but I noticed a couple of things. One young man was fascinated with the cars. He kept staring at all the Lincolns and Jaguars and Mercedes and other fancy buggies and hardly paid any attention to what the priest was saying. And after it was over, he checked out a couple of cars—walked around looking at them and peeking through the windows."

"That's more interesting than you might think," Liz said. "What else?"

"I noticed a little something between one of the women and a man. They didn't arrive together. She got out of a limo and he drove up in a Cadillac. He made a beeline for her the minute he saw her. They stood together. At one point they held hands for a few minutes."

Liz was sure Gram was talking about Miss Jane and Gus Stanky. "Was he a big man?" she asked.

"Yes. It struck me he might be one of the countess' ex-husbands—the one who used to play pro football."

Liz's instincts heightened. So, Miss Jane and the linebacker *did* have something going.

"Well, I'm going to say good-bye, dear," Gram said. "I hope I've been of some help."

"You have. Thanks Gram."

Indeed she had, Liz thought, as she hung up. The idea of Miss Jane and Gus Stanky being romantically involved put a new slant on her thinking. She recalled Fannie saying they'd helped the countess up to bed the night of her death. Was it possible they'd planned her murder, together?

What would their motive be? Had the countess found out about Miss Jane and her ex-husband and tried to break them up? Why would she do that? Jealousy, maybe? She wanted the linebacker available for escort duty. Maybe she'd threatened to cut Gus out of her will if he didn't break up with Miss Jane. Or maybe Miss Jane told Gus the countess was blackmailing her and the two of them conspired to get rid of her.

These thoughts churned round and round in her mind after she went to bed. She hadn't seen enough of Gus Stanky to form any judgments about him, but the concept of Miss Jane as a killer seemed totally out of character.

She finally got to sleep after telling herself that if she'd been able to come up with these ideas, Ike certainly had. Her last waking thought was to wish he hadn't shut her out of this case.

Chapter Nine

When Liz went into the kitchen the next morning, Fannie was unloading the dishwasher and Myrtle was at the stove. Myrtle gave her a big smile, saying, "Good morning, Ducky." Fannie promptly added her own pleasant greeting. They both seemed to be in an unusually good mood.

Then Liz remembered they were off Sundays after breakfast. She also remembered Miss Jane telling her she wouldn't have Sunday off till she'd been there a week. "I hope you two enjoy your day off," she said.

"Thanks," Fannie replied. "I'm going to my niece's in Brooklyn. I usually spend my time off with her and her family. It will be good to get out of the house. We haven't been off since Miss Harriet died."

Before Liz could ask why they hadn't gone out since the countess' death, Fannie continued. "Miss Jane said we were needed here and asked us to stay in till after the funeral, but she paid us for the time."

Myrtle frowned. "If I'd had me choice, I'd rather have gone out. I always go see me sister on me day off. She's in a nursing home in the Bronx. I'll have a visit with her awhile today, then do some shopping."

This was a new slant on Myrtle, Liz thought. "I'm sorry

your sister isn't well," she said. "How long has she been in the nursing home?"

"A few months, but she took sick two years after her husband died. That's why I left London and came to the States. But it got so I couldn't take care of her. It's Alzheimer's disease. She couldn't be left alone and I had to work, so there was nothing to do but put her in a home."

Liz felt a surge of sympathy from this poignant glimpse into Myrtle's personal life. Her feeling must have shown on her face.

"It's all right, Ducky," Myrtle said. "Thank you for caring." She turned away and busied herself at the stove.

Liz was struck with a sudden question. With Fannie and Myrtle gone for most of the day, would she be expected to cook lunch and dinner?

Myrtle provided the answer. "Sundays they always breakfast big, so they don't lunch," she said, while stirring something around with a wooden spoon in a big mixing bowl. "This morning I'm making waffles with omelets and bacon and sausages and apple biscuits and hashed brown potatoes."

And she'd do a taste test while cooking, Liz thought, plus eat generous portions of everything, later. No wonder she tipped the scales at two hundred-plus.

"Since Mr. Alistair and his family came, Miss Jane's been having tea at five on Sundays," Fannie added. "Later, they go out somewhere for dinner, so you won't have to cook for them, Beth."

"But since you're here this Sunday, Miss Jane might want you to do the tea," Myrtle said.

That would be okay, she could hack tea, Liz thought. An instant later she reconsidered. English tea was more than a cup and a crumpet.

Myrtle must have noticed her discomfort. "Don't fret, Ducks," she said. "There's enough sandwiches and meats and biscuits from last night, and plenty of cake."

"Miss Jane didn't hire you to do the meals," Fannie said.

"She might ask you to serve tea, but she'll help you get it together. She's always fair. That's Miss Jane's way."

Liz could have done without this further reminder of how nice Miss Jane was. She wasn't looking forward to telling her, today, that she was leaving tomorrow. She was going to say she called her former employer to see how she was doing, and Mrs. McGowan said she couldn't get along without her and begged her to come back.

After the Sunday breakfast routine was over, Liz was sitting at the kitchen table with a mug of coffee, when Fannie and Myrtle came out of their rooms, ready to leave, Myrtle was carrying a large shopping bag printed with a picture of the Tower of London.

"Shouldn't you be upstairs doing the bedrooms, Ducky?" Myrtle asked.

"Miss Jane told me I didn't need to go up there today till they finished getting ready for church," Liz replied.

Fannie left, but Myrtle seemed reluctant to go. She kept finding little tasks to do, like straightening the pot lids on the rack above the stove. She acted nervous, Liz thought, and she looked worried. Maybe she was worried about her sister in the nursing home and wanted to talk about it.

"Would you like to sit down with me for a few minutes, Myrtle?" she asked.

Myrtle hesitated, then shook her head. "It's not that I wouldn't like to, Ducky, but there's visiting hours where my sister is and I've stayed too long already." She picked up her purse and shopping bag and headed for the door.

"I hope you and your sister have a nice visit," Liz called after her.

Myrtle went out the door saying, "Thanks, Ducks."

Spending her day off with an Alzheimer's-stricken sister was real devotion, Liz thought, while finishing her coffee. She hoped Myrtle would get in some fun shopping after leaving the nursing home.

With no lunch or dinner to worry about, she'd have some

time to get to her notebook, she thought. Her head was bursting with questions and speculations. She wanted to get it all down before she went home tomorrow night.

Since she didn't have to change the sheets today, she'd get the bedroom routine over with quicker than yesterday. And while she was up there, she'd take another peek into the countess' bedroom, focusing on the nightstand cabinet.

She heard voices from the reception hall. The family must be gathering there, waiting for the BMW to be brought around, she decided.

She was rinsing out her coffee mug when Miss Jane came into the kitchen saying they were all leaving for church. Afterwards, the family planned to drive out to New Jersey to visit friends of Mr. Alistair's.

"I have some shopping to do after church," she said. "I'll be back here around two. The others will be back for tea around five. We'll do the tea together. After you do the bedrooms and baths, you'll be free until then, Beth. Go out if you want to. Just be sure you're back in time for tea."

Liz had no intention of going out. The idea of being alone in the house sent a tingle of excitement through her. While she was doing the upstairs rooms, she'd have time for some major snooping. But first she wanted to record her observations and speculations so she'd have a better idea what to look for.

In her room, she curled up on the bed and began to write in her notebook.

Alistair Hunterdon. He knew if his sister died first, their parents' estate would be his. Had he been in financial trouble? Was that why he came back to live in the house he'd inherited, jointly, with the countess? Fannie said he and his sister never got along. She was jealous of him and retaliated by being mean to him. Also, Dan said Alistair had objected strongly to the autopsy.

"Wow," she murmured, when she read what she'd written about Alistair. But she had much more to jot down.

Lady Sylvia. If they were having financial difficulties, she might have secretly planned to get the countess out of the way so her husband would become wealthy. Then they could return to Britain, and she'd be better able to hobnob with the likes of Queen Elizabeth.

David. Fannie said the countess had been mean to both boys. Would this, alone, be a motive for murder?

Randolph. If he really coveted the BMW and he'd developed intense hatred for his aunt because of her meanness, he could have done it, but only if his father promised him the car *before* she died. His bedroom was closest to the smoke alarm outside her room. Was he such a sound sleeper that he failed to hear it? And she'd encountered him coming out of the countess' bedroom. Though his explanation seemed believable, he might have been up to something. But what?

Miss Jane. A beneficiary? Though the countess had been treating her like dirt, she hadn't left. If the countess had been holding something over Miss Jane's head, she might have had a double motive. And how did her relationship with Gus Stanky fit in?

Gus Stanky. Most likely a beneficiary. Was he gambling again and desperate for money? And did his relationship with Miss Jane fit in anywhere? Was he aware that the countess might have something on Miss Jane? Fannie said the two of them helped get the countess to her bedroom the night of the murder.

Count Paolo Zanardi. Also a likely beneficiary. Did he need more money to support his playboy lifestyle? He'd been in the countess' bedroom that night with Gus and Miss Jane. Had he lingered after they left?

Myrtle. Only employed in the household for a couple of weeks, so wouldn't have been a beneficiary. But she and the countess had a big row and she almost quit after two days. She admitted she disliked the countess. Could her dislike have festered into homicidal hatred?

Fannie. The countess left her some money. Did Fannie know she was going to be a beneficiary? Even if she didn't, she could have had another motive. She adored Miss Jane. Did she plan the countess' death, knowing that Mr. Alistair and Lady Sylvia would ask Miss Jane to stay on and run the household?

With her observations recorded, Liz closed her notebook, locked it in the box and put the box beneath some of her clothing in a dresser drawer. While she was in the Hunterdon house she kept the key on a chain around her neck. Though chances were almost nil of the notebook being found and read by someone in the household—perhaps the killer—she wasn't risking it.

Now for her snooping. She'd start while she was straightening up Mr. Alistair's and Lady Sylvia's room. Maybe she'd come across some proof that they'd, indeed, been having money troubles. Bank statements, perhaps, or dunning letters from creditors.

But when she entered the Hunterdon's bedroom, a disheartening thought struck her. The police had most certainly searched the entire house as soon as the countess' death was declared a homicide. Ike would have latched onto any evidence of Alistair's financial status as well as possible evidence involving other household members. The field of clues had been picked clean. She might as well forget about snooping.

After she finished straightening up all the bedrooms and baths, she decided to have another peek into the countess' bedroom, anyway. She stood in the doorway, focusing on the nightstand cabinet, recalling what Dan had told her.

The substance that sent the countess into a coma was a common ingredient in household cleaner, he'd said. Since that ingredient had been found during the autopsy, he believed someone had slipped household cleaner into a booze bottle in her nightstand cabinet.

Of course the killer would have removed the incriminating bottle, she thought. It would have been long gone by the time the death was declared a homicide and the police searched the house. Ike certainly knew about this, but he hadn't been willing to discuss it with her. She sighed, wishing she could come up with something he *didn't* know.

With her next thought, she brightened. Chances were that Ike didn't know Alistair had promised Randolph the BMW. She wouldn't know about it herself if Randolph hadn't been coming on to her. If she could find out that the promise had been made *before* the countess's death, she'd have something interesting to report to Ike—a solid motive for Randolph. But the only way to find this out would be to engage Randolph in conversation. That would make it seem as if she were encouraging him. With a grimace, she told herself she had to do this if she wanted to come up with something of interest to Ike.

She glanced at her watch. It was barely noon. The Hunterdons and Miss Jane wouldn't be back for hours. She returned to her room and decided to pass the time by phoning Gram. Then she remembered Gram always went to 12 o'clock mass. She'd give her a call later.

She decided to phone Sophie. Sophie must be wondering what had happened to her. They hadn't been in touch for three days. She hadn't had time to tell Sophie she now had a cell phone.

Whether or not Sophie was on duty, she carried her own cell phone with her. As Liz punched the number, she decided she might as well let Sophie know what she'd been up to these past few days. Chances of Ike finding out through Sophie were close to zero, now. She'd be out of here and home tomorrow night and she'd tell him herself when she saw him on Tuesday.

Hearing Sophie's voice gave her a lift. She'd felt awful, keeping this from her.

"Liz! Where have you been? I called your apartment about a hundred times and no answer. And why haven't you phoned me before now?"

"It's a long and interesting story. Are you on duty? Can we talk? You're going to love what I have to tell you."

"I'm on duty but I can talk for a few minutes. Mike and I are taking a coffee break in the squad car outside a doughnut shop. What's up?"

"I'm working as a chambermaid in the home of the late Countess Zanardi. I'm alone in the house right now, so I can talk freely."

Sophie gave a squeal of delight. "You've gone undercover in the homicide house! Neat! Did you dig anything up?"

"Nothing that could send anyone to death row, but I did pick up a few things to run by Ike."

"I guess he doesn't know what you've been doing."

"Good guess. Actually, he's the reason I came up with this plan. He wouldn't let me in on anything about the case. It was almost as if he'd gone back to being Detective Sourpuss. I can't help feeling guilty about deceiving him, though."

Sophie replied with her typical logic. "His attitude left you no alternative."

This was exactly what Liz needed to hear. It eased some of her guilt.

"How long are you going to be there?" Sophie asked.

"Till tomorrow night . . ." Just then Liz heard footsteps in the kitchen. "Sophie, I think there's someone in the kitchen. Everybody's supposed be gone for hours. Will you hold while I go and have a look?"

"Sure, I'll hang on."

Liz thrust the phone into her apron pocket and went down the hall. Entering the kitchen, she was surprised to see Randolph walking towards her. The family must have decided not to drive out to New Jersey after all. Though it seemed out of character, he must have come to the kitchen looking for something to eat.

"Mr. Randolph! I thought you were all going to New Jersey after church."

"I begged off," he said. "After church I told them I had a bad headache, so they brought me home." His smile was close enough to a leer to indicate his headache was phony and his family had gone to New Jersey, anyway. She was alone in the house with this wannabe womanizer.

"Oh, I'm sorry you're not feeling well, Mr. Randolph," she said. She almost added, "What can I do for you?" but decided this might be a poor choice of words.

He stepped closer to her. "I knew you were here alone and I thought we could have some fun."

She recalled her plan to encourage him as a means of finding out when his father had promised him the BMW. But she was not about to promote the kind of fun his leer suggested. She'd have to scrap the plan.

She turned away from him, saying, "I couldn't have fun with a child of my employer."

Talk about a poor choice of words! She'd only intended to take the wind out of this callow Captain Casanova's sails by referring to his youth and reminding him that she was a family servant. Instead, he reacted with anger at this slur on his budding manhood. His eyes flashed. Muttering an oath, he grabbed her and planted a clumsy kiss on her mouth.

"I'll show you I'm no child!" he bellowed. He took hold of her shoulders and began to shove her down the hall towards her bedroom.

Her temper flared. "Take your hands off me, you creep," she bellowed in return, trying to wrest free.

It wasn't until he pushed her into her room and slammed the door that she knew for sure she was in trouble. But before her temper dissolved into fear, she remembered the cell phone in her pocket. Sophie said she'd hang on. The Hunterdon home was in Sophie's precinct. If Sophie could hear what was happening, she and her partner could be here in a few minutes.

Meanwhile, if this big Brit boy was in earnest about showing her he was no child, she wasn't going to make it easy for him. Pop had taught her some self-defense moves. She kneed him in the groin. He yelped in pain. Temporarily immobilized, he relaxed his hold on her. She broke away and ran for the door, hoping to make it to the kitchen and out the service entrance. But she'd barely made it halfway down the hall when he came after her and dragged her back into the bedroom.

She tried the self-defense tactic again, but this time he was wary and warded it off. Before he could give her another clumsy kiss, she started yelling at him, hoping Sophie had stayed on the line.

"Let go of me, you punk kid! Wait till your father hears about this! Fat chance you'll have of getting that BMW now!"

This might divert him, if only briefly, she thought. It did. Mention of the coveted BMW stopped him in his tracks for a minute, before he yelled back at her. "It will be my word against yours, and my father isn't going to believe *you*!"

Through their yelling came the sound of a doorbell.

"Someone's at the service door," Liz said. *Sophie and Mike to the rescue?*

"When nobody answers, whoever it is will go away," Randolph mumbled. He planted another oafish kiss on her mouth. She'd been kissed by enough men to realize this kid hadn't done much of it. That didn't make him any less of a threat, though. The idea that she considered him a child had really rallied his hormones.

But hope that help was at hand gave her extra strength. She managed to fend him off, and was just about to poke her fingers into his eyes when an explosive banging, creaking sound halted all the action.

"What in bloody hell was that?" Randolph muttered.

He'd barely spoken when the bedroom door burst open. Liz thought she'd never again see so beautiful a sight as Sophie and her partner standing there, guns drawn.

Chapter Ten

Sophie rushed to her side, her face etched with concern. "Are you okay ma'am?"

Ma'am! It took a moment for Liz to realize Sophie didn't want to blow her cover.

"A little shook up but otherwise fine, Officer," she replied, going along with Sophie. She lowered her voice to a whisper. "When I realized what was shaping up, I wasn't sure we were still connected, or if we were, I didn't know if you could hear what was happening."

"Even before you started hollering, I heard enough to know you were in trouble," Sophie whispered back.

The three of them looked at Randolph. He'd dropped Liz like a hot potato the instant he saw the uniforms and guns. He was now cowering in a corner, evidently too scared to wonder how these two cops knew what was going on in the Hunterdon house.

He reminded Liz of the little boy caught with his hand in the cookie jar. She might have felt sorry for him, if she hadn't been the cookie he'd been groping for.

Mike holstered his gun and approached him, issuing the routine instructions before a weapons and drugs check. When he asked for ID, Randolph looked so chastened that Liz thought he was going to burst into tears. How quickly he'd changed from macho man to a kid who didn't want his father to find out what had happened.

Mike eyed the ID. "Randolph Hunterdon!" he exclaimed. "This guy's not an intruder, Sophie, he lives here."

"That doesn't give him the right to assault me," Liz said.

"Don't get your Irish up," Sophie replied. "Mike only meant since this guy didn't break into the house, instead of unlawful entry and assault, the charge will be just assault."

"I'll read him his rights and we'll take him over to the station house and file the complaint," Mike said.

All Liz could think of at that moment was Ike finding out about this. Even if he wasn't in the squad room when Randolph was brought in, almost everyone at the station house, from rookie cops to veteran detectives, knew Pop. Many of them knew *her* from the days when Pop used to bring her into the station house—a teenaged kid hooked on homicides. It wouldn't take long for the word to get around that Frank Rooney's daughter had been assaulted. She couldn't have Ike find out what she'd been up to this weekend before she had a chance to tell him.

"I don't want to file a complaint," she said.

Sophie and Mike stared at her. "Are you serious?" Mike asked. Sophie didn't say anything. Liz was sure Sophie knew she was serious, and why.

"I believe this was a one-time thing. I made a remark that got his dander up," Liz said.

Mike shook his head in disapproval. "Sounds like you're letting this kid off by blaming yourself."

Before she could think of a reply, another thought flashed into her mind. She turned to Randolph, who was still shamefaced, but starting to look relieved. "I'll make you a deal," she said. "I won't file charges against you if you tell me something."

"I'll tell you anything I can," he replied, his voice shaking. "Just so my father doesn't find out about this."

The feeling struck her that even if Sophie hadn't overheard the ruckus over the phone, she might have gotten out of this predicament, anyway. A few more references to the BMW would have been like cold water on the idea of having fun with the chambermaid.

"When did your father promise you the BMW?" she asked. She knew the question might make him suspicious but she hoped he was too worried about his father finding out what he'd done to think of anything else.

His prompt reply indicated she was right. "The day after we arrived in New York."

"After you saw the car?"

"Yes. We drove to church in it. Father knew I was impressed with it the minute I saw it. He told me it was part of my grandparents' estate and when my aunt died it would be his. Then he told me when that happened he planned to get a Jaguar and he'd give me the BMW."

This statement seemed to cast as much suspicion on Alistair as on Randolph, Liz thought. Perhaps more. If Randolph was the guilty one, would he have been dumb enough to admit he'd been promised the car before his aunt's death?

"Are you absolutely sure you want to let this guy off?" Mike asked.

Liz nodded. Every instinct told her that Randolph would not pull another such move towards some other girl. He was just a kid whose testosterone had been jazzed up by her remark about him being a child.

"Yes I do," she replied. "Thanks for your help officers."

"I don't like leaving you alone with this character." Sophie said.

Randolph spoke up, his voice still shaky. "I know I acted like the worst kind of cad. I'm sorry, Beth. I don't know what came over me."

Sophie cast him an angry look. "Don't let it come over you again. You lucked out this time."

"We'll be cruising this area for a while, and we just might decide to stop by again," Mike warned.

While they all walked down the hall towards the kitchen, Mike said they'd have to file a police report on the incident.

Liz looked at Sophie. She knew Sophie would pick up what she was thinking. *Ike might hear about it.*

"Yes, we must file a report," Sophie said, with a wink.

The wink told Liz that Sophie's report would be filed as a trivial incident, something unlikely to attract attention at the station house.

In the kitchen, the sight of the service door sagging off its hinges with screws bent and dangling, evoked a wail from Randolph. He turned to Liz. "We have to get the door repaired before my father comes home."

"What do you mean, *we?*" Liz asked.

"Yeah," Mike said. "Mr. Hunterdon, I suggest you find some new screws and a screwdriver and get busy." With that, he and Sophie stepped around the sagging door and left.

Liz felt no qualms about being left alone with Randolph. He knew he had to remove all evidence of the incident to keep his father from finding out what had happened. That, alone, would have quelled any lingering idea of having fun with the servant girl.

But had this uppercrust Brit boy ever held a screwdriver in his hand? If he hadn't, she might have to help him. For both their sakes, the door had to be back on its hinges before Miss Jane returned at 2 o'clock. "Have you ever fixed anything before?" she asked.

"Nothing quite like this, but I'll give it a try," he replied, looking uncertain. "Are there any tools around here?"

Liz couldn't imagine a household not having a few basic tools on hand, even a house like this one. "They're probably in one of the cabinet drawers," she replied. But she wasn't going to help him find them. She sat down at the table and watched him search.

A grunt of satisfaction told her he'd found the tool drawer. Holding a battery-powered screwdriver and a packet of large screws, he approached the door.

She knew she could have helped by bracing the door for him. He knew better than to ask for her assistance. Lucky for him he was a big, strong kid and he managed to get the door in position for drilling the screws.

She had to admit the job turned out better than she'd expected. The door looked as if it would hold.

"Do you think anyone will notice the slight damage around the hinges and the chipped paint?" he asked, putting the drill back in the drawer.

"If I didn't know what happened, I wouldn't notice it," she replied. She eyed the floor around the door, littered with old screws, slivers of wood and paint chips. "But you'd better find a broom and sweep up this mess."

He located a broom and dustpan, and got to work. After he dumped the debris into a trash basket under the sink, he looked at her with a sheepish smile. "You've been a good sport, Beth, a real brick."

Let him think what he would. No need for him to know she'd been self-serving when she let him off the hook.

She checked her watch. "Miss Jane will be back soon," she said. "She'll come to the kitchen to let me know she's here. You'd better get up to your room."

He nodded. Like an obedient child, he started up the stairs.

As she watched him go, she thought of all the other predicaments she'd gotten into while doing her own homicide investigations. Ike never let up reminding her how lucky she'd been to have emerged from them virtually unscathed. She wasn't looking forward to telling him about this one. For a moment, she thought about leaving out the Randolph incident when she told Ike where she'd been all weekend. But that would be almost the same as another lie, and she never wanted to lie to him again.

Back in her room, she phoned Gram to tell her she was giving notice today and she'd be home tomorrow night.

"I hope you picked up lots of information," Gram said.

"I did, but I don't know if it's anything Ike hasn't found out himself."

"Oh, speaking of Ike, he phoned here this morning, wanting to speak to you. I told him you were out doing some shopping for me. He asked how I was feeling. I said much better."

Now she had Gram lying, too, Liz thought, with a pang of guilt.

"He wants you to call him on his cell phone," Gram went on. "We better hang up so you can do that before he thinks I didn't give you the message."

"Okay. Thanks, Gram." She hung up the phone, feeling slightly ill. She couldn't tell Ike over the telephone what she'd planned to tell him in person. Depending on how their conversation went when she called him, she might have to continue her lies.

She punched his number. He answered with a terse, "Eichle."

"Ike, it's Liz. Gram said you called."

"Liz . . . yes, I phoned this morning."

He was wondering why it had taken her so long to get back to him, she thought. She felt mired in lies. She wasn't going to make it worse with a fabricated excuse. "Sorry I didn't call earlier," she said. At least that was the truth.

"I just wanted to say hello and tell you I'll see you Tuesday night," he said.

She knew she couldn't wait till Tuesday night to unburden herself. "I'll be home tomorrow night. Can you make it, then? I have something I really need to tell you."

"Sounds serious."

"It is. Please say you can come over tomorrow night."

"Okay, what time?"

She did some quick calculating. When she told Miss Jane she was leaving, she'd say she'd stay through tomorrow's dinner. "I'll be home by eight-thirty," she replied.

"I'll see you then," he said. "And by the way, I've missed you."

"I've missed you too."

She said good-bye, thankful that she'd managed to get through the conversation without any more lies, and with a parting statement so true it brought a lump into her throat.

Now she wished Miss Jane would come back. She wanted to get the unpleasant task of giving notice over with. It was almost 2 o'clock. To pass the time, she turned on her radio. It seemed like ages since she'd heard a news broadcast. She didn't know what was going on with the Zanardi homicide investigation.

Nothing much had happened. News of the toxic substance found during the countess' autopsy was still being withheld. Did Ike know that nobody in the Hunterdon household believed the death was a homicide? Had he gotten wind of Alistair Hunterdon's move to have this reversed? She had so much to tell him. But she knew she had to come clean about her weekend caper before she got around to telling him what she'd picked up.

The sound of Miss Jane's voice penetrated her thoughts. "Beth, I'm back."

Liz switched off the radio and hurried to the kitchen. Now would be the time for her to break the news that she was leaving.

A sudden thought sprang into her mind. Randolph's assault on her would be a better reason for quitting her job than returning to her previous one. But she discarded the idea. She'd made a deal with Randolph. She couldn't go back on her word even though he deserved it.

"I have to tell you something, Miss Jane," she said.

She knew her face must have betrayed her discomfort when Miss Jane sat down at the table with a sigh, saying, "You look upset and uncomfortable, Beth. I hope I'm wrong, but I think I know what you're going to tell me. The job isn't working out for you, is it? You're not going to stay with us."

Liz nodded. "But it's not the job, ma'am, it's Mrs. McGowan. I phoned her today to see how she's getting along and she told me she changed her mind and wants me back. She needs me."

"I know you were happy with Mrs. McGowan and it's understandable you want to go back to her," Miss Jane said. "We'll be sorry to lose you, Beth. You were doing a good job. When do you plan to leave us?"

This was awful, Liz thought. She felt terrible, doing this to Miss Jane. She blurted it out. "Mrs. McGowan wants me right away."

Miss Jane looked startled. "Right away? Surely you don't mean today."

Slightly relieved, Liz shook her head. "Not today. I'll stay till after dinner tomorrow night. I'm sorry, ma'am."

"I know you are, Beth. And thank you for staying through tomorrow. I can call the employment agency the next day."

"I hope it won't take long for you to get someone," Liz said. She was thinking of Myrtle, again balking at having to do what she considered menial work.

"I'm sure it won't," Miss Jane replied. "I'll figure out what we owe you for your three days and give you your check tomorrow." She smiled and patted Liz's hand. "You were here for us at a very difficult time, Beth. I honestly don't know how we would have managed without you."

She rose from her chair, saying she was going to her room. "I'll come down around four and we'll start getting tea together," she said.

This woman was close to being a saint, Liz thought. How could the countess have treated her so shabbily? And why had Miss Jane put up with it?

The question surrounding Miss Jane was still in her mind while she took a shower and changed into her serving uniform for tea. It seemed as much of a mystery as who'd planned the countess' murder. She was still puzzling over it when Miss Jane came down to the kitchen.

"It's lucky we have plenty of food left over from yesterday," Miss Jane said, as they arranged sandwiches on a platter. "Mr. Alistair's New Jersey friends probably offered refreshments during the afternoon, but I think we'd better have tea ready for them soon after they get home. I know the boys will be hungry."

"Oh," Liz said. "Mr. Randolph didn't go to New Jersey. He wasn't feeling well, he said. He went to his room to rest."

Miss Jane looked surprised. "He seemed perfectly fine when I left them after church."

"He said he had a headache."

Miss Jane nodded. "Headaches can come on suddenly. Lucky they were still in the city so they could just drop him off."

Voices from upstairs indicated that the family was home. Miss Jane went up to the dining room to set the tea table. "We won't bother with the silver tea service today since it's just family," she said, as she ascended the stairs. "We'll use the Meissen."

Liz took the china tea service down from the cupboard, then put the water on to boil and started loading food onto the dumbwaiter. She was getting pretty good at this, she thought. Her immigrant great-grandmother would be proud of her.

When the family and Miss Jane were seated in the dining room, Liz saw Lady Sylvia look across the table at Randolph. "Headache all better Randy darling?" Her voice sounded like dialogue from a British film.

"Yes, better, thanks Mummy," he replied.

"Too bad you didn't come with us," David said. "Father's friends have two keen looking daughters."

"Perhaps it's just as well you didn't meet those lovely girls, Randy," Alistair said, in a joking tone. "We wouldn't see much of you around here. You'd be off to New Jersey in the BMW."

"When are you turning the BMW over to him, Father?" David asked.

"As soon as my Jaguar is delivered," Alistair replied.

Randolph made no comment. Liz knew he must be thinking he'd almost blown his chance to have the BMW. He remained silent and subdued as he drank his tea and packed away several hearty sandwiches, some biscuits with jam, and a wedge of chocolate cake.

After tea, when Liz had finished clearing the kitchen, she went to her room to record the day's events in her notebook. She decided not to write anything about the Randolph incident. It didn't have anything to do with solving the case, but she was sure the questions about Miss Jane did.

She was still puzzling over Miss Jane when she went upstairs to turn down the beds and make sure the bathrooms were in order for the evening. After attending to the adults' rooms, she did David's room and gave the boys' bathroom a few wipes. She deliberately skipped Randolph's room. There was no way he'd complain to Miss Jane that the chambermaid hadn't turned down his bed, plumped up his pillows and laid out his robe.

Back in the kitchen, she decided to take a good look at the service door. She hadn't examined it closely, nor had she tested it to see if it opened and closed properly.

On close scrutiny, it was obvious something had happened to it. Not only did it look scruffy around the hinges, but also it didn't open without some pressure. Fannie and Myrtle might have trouble unlocking it when they came back tonight. They'd probably mention it to Miss Jane. Would Miss Jane come and look at it and think someone had tried to break in by jimmying the door? Would the police be summoned? Again, she felt the threat of Ike finding out what she'd been doing, before she could tell him, herself.

She lay in bed, listening to her radio, trying not to be paranoid about the door, when she heard someone come into the kitchen. It had to be Fannie or Myrtle. Had there been any problem with the door? She got out of bed, opened her door and saw Fannie coming down the corridor.

"Hi," she said. "Did you have a nice day?"

"Very nice, thank you, Beth."

She waited for Fannie to say something about the service door not working right. Fannie said nothing, but she had to make sure. "By the way," she said, "I went out in the service yard for a breath of air this afternoon and when I came back in I had trouble opening the door. I had to push hard before it would open. Did you notice anything?"

"Now that you mention it, I had a little trouble getting my key to work, and then I had to push hard too," Fannie replied. "I guess we should tell Miss Jane about it tomorrow so she can call the handyman."

Liz went back to bed, still worrying that this would be reported to the police. In the less than twenty-four hours before she saw Ike, he could get wind of an attempted break-in at the Hunterdon address. He might suspect a possible connection to the murder and he'd come over to investigate. He'd want to question everyone in the house, including Beth, the new maid.

If she'd been able to fall asleep she would have been awakened by the loud creaking noise in the kitchen an hour or so later. *The door!* She jumped out of bed, threw on her robe and raced down the corridor.

She and Fannie had left a light on in the kitchen for Myrtle. In its glow, like someone in a bizarre theater scene, a startled Myrtle stood with several parcels strewn around her feet, her shoulder still braced against the partly unhinged and sagging door.

Chapter Eleven

The expression in Myrtle's watery blue eyes went from startled to embarrassed. Her face flushed. "The bloody door gave way on me," she said.

Liz noticed she didn't mention having to push hard to get the door open. And there was no mistaking her humiliation. She believed she'd caused the damage all by herself.

Eyeing the parcels strewn on the floor, Liz decided that Myrtle must have had her arms full and shouldered her way in. Two hundred pounds of pressure had been too much for the weakened hinges. For an instant, she thought about letting Myrtle assume the blame. That would put an end to her worries about the police being called to investigate a break-in. Miss Jane would believe Myrtle was responsible.

She couldn't do it. "It wasn't your fault, Myrtle," she said. "That door was ready to fall down before you even put your key in the lock."

Still shamefaced, Myrtle looked at her, shaking her head. "You're being kind, Ducky. I know what happened. With me arms full, I had to crump me way in. Me being too heavy done it." She shook her head again. "I thought I knew why I was getting so heavy. I thought it was me prescription medicine making me want to eat too much. I cut down the doses some weeks ago, but it didn't help.

Starting tomorrow, I'm using me will power to cut down on me food."

Liz thought Myrtle's flushed face suggested her medication might be for high blood pressure. Before she could tell Myrtle it wasn't a good idea to reduce doses of prescribed medicine, Fannie appeared, wearing nightgown and robe.

"What was that noise I heard?" she asked. Then her eyes took in the listing door and Myrtle gathering up her parcels.

Liz rushed to explain. "Myrtle was carrying a bunch of packages and she had to shove the door open with her shoulder and some hinges pulled out. I tried to tell her there was something wrong with the door, but she thinks she's to blame."

She waited for Fannie to back her up about the faulty door. Instead, Fannie said, "Don't worry about it, Myrtle. Miss Jane will call the handyman tomorrow and have the door fixed."

Liz gave Fannie a sharp glance. Fannie evaded eye contact and turned to go back to her room. Fannie was getting even with Myrtle for her high and mighty attitude, Liz thought. She had an instant of indecision before deciding to let things go at that. Except for Myrtle's embarrassment, no harm had been done, and for her, only good had come out of it.

Myrtle finished gathering up her parcels and placed them on the kitchen table. She cast a worried look at the door. "It shouldn't be left like that all night," she said. "I'll move something over to prop it up." She looked around. "It should be something heavy."

Liz had no doubt that Myrtle could haul the washing machine or dryer out of the laundry room and shove it across the kitchen if she decided to.

"No need for that, Myrtle," she said, opening the tool drawer. "I can get the hinges back on temporarily if you'll help me."

Myrtle nodded. "Of course I'll help you, Ducky. Just tell me what you want me to do."

Two hundred pounds braced against the door made the job easy. This second unhinging wasn't as damaging as the first. Liz couldn't find any new screws, but the ones Randolph had used looked okay. She felt satisfied that the reinstalled hinges would hold till the handyman came.

Liz was testing Myrtle's key in the lock, with Myrtle standing by, watching, when a voice sounded from the service yard. "Myrtle? Is something wrong? Looks like you're having trouble with the door."

Liz turned to confront a big, Hispanic-looking man wearing the semblance of a uniform. She recalled Miss Jane mentioning a private security guard who patrolled the block.

"Everything's all right, Mr. Romero," Myrtle replied. Her voice sounded as if she were embarrassed all over again. She gestured towards Liz. "This here's our new maid, Beth."

The guard stepped closer. Liz knew he couldn't miss signs of her repair job.

"What happened here?" he asked.

"It wasn't an attempted break in, if that's what you're thinking," Liz replied. "A couple of hinges pulled away when Myrtle got home a little while ago and opened the door. We just finished fixing it when you came along."

The guard's eyes shifted from the hinges to Myrtle. Liz saw him bite at his lip. "I see," he said, turning away. Liz knew he was trying to hold back a laugh. Myrtle must have known it too. She looked as if she wanted to sink through the floor.

"Well, as long as there's nothing wrong, I'll be going," the guard said. He hastened out to his car parked at the curb.

Liz closed the door and locked it. "I guess we're both ready for some sleep," she said, putting the tools away. She knew she'd have no problem drifting off, now.

Myrtle gathered her packages from the kitchen table and handed one of them to Liz. "Here, Ducks," she said. "I bought meself a box of chocolates but you can have them. After what happened tonight I'm swearing off sweets. When a body leans on a door and the door gives way, it's a sign."

Liz was the first one in the kitchen the next morning. She'd wakened much earlier than usual after a deep, untroubled sleep. It would be a while before Fannie and Myrtle appeared, she thought, looking at the kitchen clock.

She made coffee and sat down at the table. What a great feeling, knowing this was her last day here. Had it been worth the effort? She wasn't sure, yet. She believed that some of the information she'd picked up would help Ike, but he might already be aware of it, or he might not consider it worth a second thought. Tonight, she'd know.

While drinking her coffee, she glanced at the service door. Poor Myrtle must have been mortified, especially when the guard had to be told what happened. But Miss Jane would be kind and understanding, and she'd never suspect the hinges were already loose before Myrtle heaved her weight against the door. Besides herself, nobody except Randolph knew what actually happened, and neither of them would ever tell.

Watching a member of Britain's nobility sweep up debris from the kitchen floor had been an amusing experience. He'd have done anything to keep his father from finding out the circumstances leading to the damaged door. She imagined Lady Sylvia's reaction if she had seen her darling Randy wielding broom and dustpan and emptying the chips of wood and paint and the bent screws into the wastebasket under the sink.

All that debris was still in the basket, right there where Myrtle could see it when she came into the kitchen. In the second unhinging, the screws had come out without making a mess. Myrtle would remember they hadn't swept the floor afterwards. Myrtle was no dummy. If she saw the telltale vestiges of the first unhinging in the wastebasket, she'd know she'd been had.

She took the wastebasket to the outside receptacle and emptied it. She'd just put it back under the sink when Fannie and Myrtle appeared. They both glanced at the door. Myrtle looked pleased that it hadn't fallen down during the night. Fannie looked surprised, as if she'd expected to find it still hanging off its hinges.

"Who fixed the door?" Fannie asked.

"Myrtle and I did," Liz replied. "We couldn't leave it open like that all night." She had ambivalent feelings towards Fannie this morning. She was annoyed at her for not coming out and telling Myrtle the truth about the door, yet she was thankful for her silence. In a way, she was being as untruthful as Fannie, she thought, but the small pang of guilt she felt was outweighed by her peace of mind.

The daily routine began. Liz realized this was the last time she'd watch Myrtle prepare breakfast. She noticed that Myrtle refrained from sampling two or three of her freshly baked blueberry muffins before they were loaded onto the dumbwaiter. Also, she didn't put four spoonfuls of sugar into her tea. She was in earnest when she said she'd received a sign telling her to go on a diet.

Funny how events linked up to one another, Liz thought. If it hadn't been for randy Randolph wanting to have a fling with the chambermaid, fat Myrtle would not have decided she must lose weight.

During the lull before lunch, when she and Fannie and Myrtle were together in the kitchen, she knew she had to tell them she was leaving.

"There's something you should know," she said. "I'm leaving tonight."

Fannie's voice sounded shocked. "Leaving? For good?"

"Yes, after dinner."

"Why?" Myrtle asked, frowning.

"The lady I worked for before wants me back."

"Does Miss Jane know?" Fannie asked.

"Sure. I told her yesterday."

Myrtle looked at Fannie with a scowl. "So it's to be just you and me again."

"Miss Jane will find someone else soon," Fannie replied. "It will be easy now that Miss Harriet's gone."

Myrtle leveled her watery blue eyes on Liz. "I hope she finds someone as nice as you, Ducky. I don't mind saying I'll miss having you around. It's not often I take a shine to someone."

Evidently it wasn't often that someone praised Myrtle's culinary skills and went along with her bragging, Liz thought.

After lunch Fannie said she had to do laundry and Myrtle said she was going to her room to rest. Again, Fannie remarked that she was never caught up. "It never ends," she grumbled. "There's a whole new pile since this morning, and the dryer's full from yesterday's load. Would you mind emptying the dryer and doing the folding?"

"Of course I wouldn't mind," Liz said. "Anyway, that's one of my duties."

"I didn't know if you'd do it, this being your last day," Fannie replied. She sighed. "If Myrtle would help me once in a while instead of sitting on her royal rump, I could get caught up. I do all her things, and believe me she goes through a mountain of uniforms and aprons and underwear, besides her towels and her bed sheets. She acts like I'm her personal washerwoman."

"Have you thought of holding back on Myrtle's things?" Liz asked. "That might help you get caught up. And maybe when she notices she's running low on clean things, she'll take the hint and do her own wash."

"I promised Miss Jane . . ." Fannie began. Then she nodded. "I'll try it, this once." She scooped up a large heap of soiled articles, including a white towel with Myrtle's identifying green stripe, a white uniform the size of a tent and two food-stained aprons. "These are all Myrtle's," she said, tossing the whole lot into a basket on the floor. "They can stay there a couple of days and we'll see what happens."

Liz felt as if she'd done her good deed for the day. She hoped this wouldn't cause further friction between Fannie and Myrtle, but if it did, she wouldn't know about it. The thought of going home tonight brought on a smile.

Later, in her room, she phoned Sophie. She knew Sophie must be wondering what happened after she and Mike left yesterday. In all the excitement, she'd neglected to give Sophie her new cell phone number.

"Any more trouble with Randolph?" Sophie asked.

"None. He hasn't given me so much as a glance since last night. All he has on his mind is keeping his father from finding out."

Sophie laughed. "Mike and I were pretty sure of that. But we got talking and we agreed the kid might not know the difference between a hammer and a screwdriver and we shouldn't have walked out and left the door hanging off the hinges. So we cruised by the house a little later and saw the door was up. Then we saw a woman get out of a taxi and go in the front door. I told Mike she was probably Miss Jane, the friend of Countess Zanardi's, and we knew you wouldn't be alone in the house with the oversexed kid. When are you going home?"

"Tonight. Ike's coming over at eight-thirty."

"Are you going to tell him . . . oops, I gotta go, Liz. I'll phone you tomorrow at your office."

While going through the evening bedroom routine, Liz again took pleasure in skipping Randolph's room. Instead, she opened the door to the countess' bedroom for a parting look at the scene of the crime.

She stood in the doorway, looking at the nightstand, imagining the countess reaching into the cabinet for her liquor bottle. Just one more drink . . .

Someone in the household knew it would be her last drink. Like Dan, she believed the countess' last drink had been taken from a vodka bottle laced with household cleaner. She pictured that person stealing into the countess' bedroom later, knowing she'd gone into a coma, staging the smoking-in-bed scenario, then removing the bottle. As she asked herself *who?* she felt the familiar kindling of her imagination. Her wildfire imagination, Pop called it. Once it took hold, there was no stopping it.

Possibilities sparked her mind. Questions flared. Though it was likely the bottle had been taken out of the house and disposed of immediately after the crime was committed, maybe this hadn't happened. Maybe the killer hid the bottle somewhere in the house, waiting for an opportune time to get rid of it. Suppose it was still in its hiding place when the police searched the house. What if it was so well hidden that they overlooked it? *What if the bottle was still in the house?*

She tried to douse the concept with logic. A killer would have to be half-brained not to get rid of the incriminating bottle quickly, even if the death was first believed to be an accident. But she couldn't get this notion out of her mind. Absurd as it was, the idea of the bottle still being somewhere in the house persisted.

She was about to turn away from the countess' bedroom and close the door when she recalled her encounter with Randolph right here, on her first day as Beth. He'd said he'd been using the countess' bathroom and he'd rushed past her with barely a glance.

What if Randolph were the killer and he hadn't had the opportunity to dispose of the bottle somewhere away from the house? She could almost hear Lady Sylvia's voice: "Now, Randy, darling, your father and I don't want you or David going out alone. Until you become familiar with New York, you must always go out together and stay together."

That would mean Randolph was stuck with keeping the bottle in the house. What if he'd gotten apprehensive about hiding it in one place all the time? What if he'd been switching it around? What if he'd hidden it in the countess' bedroom and decided to change the hiding place again, that morning? Maybe he had it on him when he rushed past her. She'd thought he was on his way to breakfast, but he could have gone to his room and re-hidden the bottle. It was possible he'd changed the hiding place again by now.

She closed the bedroom door, but she couldn't close down her thoughts. Where would Randolph have stashed the bottle the last time he changed the hiding place?

Before she could dismiss the question and tell herself to forget this crazy idea, a possible answer ignited her mind. Randolph was in the kitchen on Sunday, and he'd been walking towards her *from the direction of the storeroom!* He could have hidden the bottle in there! The storeroom would be a perfect hiding place.

Knowing how farfetched this was could not keep her from deciding to have a look around the storeroom. She hurried down the corridor to the back stairs, praying that Fannie and Myrtle wouldn't be in the kitchen. They weren't. She could go in there without having to come up with a reason. She went in and closed the door.

Undaunted by the array of boxes on the shelves, she began to search. After rummaging through cartons of blankets smelling of mothballs, and boxes of linens, draperies and curtains, she opened a large box of Christmas decorations. While she looked through a dozen or so small boxes of tree ornaments and delved through an assortment of wreaths and garlands, her fired-up imagination began to cool down.

Just as she started thinking she was wasting her time, she remembered something Pop once told her: *"Go with your hunches."* Was her idea about the storeroom a hunch? Whatever it was, it had taken her too far for her to turn back. She continued her search through layers of Christmas decorations.

Seconds later she came to the bottom of the box and found a package wrapped in newspaper and tied with twine.

Excitement jabbed at her heart. The shape and size of the parcel looked as if it could contain a bottle.

But the shape and size of the parcel also suggested it could be a Christmas figurine—a Santa Claus, maybe, wrapped carefully to prevent breakage. There was only one way to find out. She'd unwrap it here. If it turned out to be a Christmas figurine, she'd re-wrap it and put it back. If the package contained a bottle, she'd take it with her when she went home, tonight, and give it to Ike.

But would she have time to unwrap the parcel before Fannie and Myrtle came into the kitchen? They'd be curious if they saw her coming out of the storeroom with a package. They might think she'd stolen something.

She opened the door a wide crack. Nobody was in the kitchen. But Fannie and Myrtle might appear any minute. She decided to take the parcel to her room while the coast was still clear. She could open it there. If it wasn't the bottle, she'd get it back to the storeroom, somehow.

Clutching the parcel, she scurried across the kitchen and down the hall to her room. After she closed the door she began to feel foolish. All this for what was probably a Santa Claus figurine. Well, she'd soon know.

Just as she reached to undo the twine, a knock sounded on her door, followed by Miss Jane's voice. "Beth, I want to give you your check."

Liz dropped the package into her tote bag and opened the door.

"I'm sorry you're leaving us," Miss Jane said, handing her an envelope. "If you ever need a job, be sure and let me know."

"Thank you, Miss Jane," Liz said, feeling guilty and awkward, But Miss Jane eased the moment with a warm smile and a pat on Liz's shoulder before leaving. For an instant, Liz recalled her suspicions regarding Miss Jane. They'd been as strong as the feelings she now had about Randolph. But she couldn't dwell on Miss Jane now. This situation with the package was too important.

She looked at the check. Her Irish immigrant great-grandmother would have worked a year for what Beth earned in three days.

She put the check in her purse and had just taken the parcel out of her tote bag, when another knock sounded on her door. It was Fannie, asking Beth if she was ready to help set up the dining room for dinner.

"I was just about to change into my serving uniform. I'll see you in the dining room in a few minutes," Liz replied. Once more, she returned the parcel to her tote bag. Opening it would have to wait till after dinner. She told herself, again, it probably contained a Santa Claus figurine.

The dinner routine seemed to drag, but at last it ended and she went to her room. She'd almost finished her packing. She'd say good-bye to Fannie and Myrtle on her way out. There was nothing to stop her from opening the package now.

She was taking it out of her tote bag when she noticed the date on the newspaper wrapping. She stared at it, stunned. *This was last Thursday's newspaper!* A Christmas decoration would have been wrapped in a paper from December or January. Now she knew beyond a doubt there wasn't a Santa Claus figurine in there.

She started to pick at the twine, her hands trembling from excitement, when a sudden thought halted her. The killer's fingerprints might be on the bottle. She shouldn't risk disturbing the wrapping and perhaps smudging the prints. She should leave the package unwrapped, take it home and have Ike open it when he came over tonight. He'd know how to handle it.

It took all of her willpower, but she put the package back in her tote bag, unopened. She finished her packing, then went to say good-bye to Fannie and Myrtle. On her way out the service door, she said good-bye to Beth the chambermaid. She was herself again, and soon she'd be back in her own apartment, presenting Ike with evidence which would help him solve the case.

But before she gave him the package to open, she wanted to get her confession over with. She didn't want to get him all pleased and appreciative and then hit him with where she'd been all weekend. When she followed up her confession with this important evidence, chances were he'd forgive her.

Chapter Twelve

She'd taken a taxi because of her suitcase and the tote bag. As the cab approached her building, she felt her heart quicken—mostly from apprehension, she told herself. Much as she wanted to see Ike, she dreaded his reaction when she told him she'd lied to him.

When the cab drew up in front of her building, she saw Ike's car and Ike standing on the sidewalk. When she got out, he walked towards her, calling, "Hello."

"Have you been waiting long?" she called back.

"Only a few minutes. I phoned you from out here and when there was no answer I figured you'd show up soon."

By now they were face to face. He gave her a hug and a kiss. She wondered if there'd be any more hugs and kisses after she told him where she'd been all weekend.

She noticed him looking curiously at the plain skirt and blouse she had on. Not exactly her style. Fortunately, she'd let her hair loose from the unbecoming ponytail.

He took her suitcase and tote bag and they climbed the steps to the building entrance. "I think the Moscarettis are out," he said. "I didn't see their curtain twitching."

Inside, Liz glanced at Rosa's and Joe's door. When it didn't open, she knew Ike was right. Good, she thought. She didn't want to spend even a few minutes talking to

Rosa tonight. She wanted to get up to her apartment and unburden her conscience.

"How's your grandmother?" he asked, as she unlocked her door.

It was difficult coming up with a reply that wasn't yet another lie. She put together a truthful answer. "Oh, Gram's all right."

"I thought she sounded fine when I talked to her on the phone," he said. "Where do you want these bags?"

"Just set the suitcase over by the closet." She glanced at the tote bag. "I'll take the little one. There's something in it I want you to look at." It was all she could do to keep from whipping out the parcel and begging him to open it without delay.

He handed her the tote bag, then sat down on the sofa, stretching his long legs out as he always did. She put the bag at the other end of the sofa. "I'll make coffee," she said, going behind the screen to the kitchenette.

"Shall I have a look at what's in the bag?" he asked.

"Not yet. I have a lot to tell you first."

He nodded. "Something serious you really needed to tell me, you said on the phone."

He seemed subdued—not quite like himself, she thought. Or maybe it was only her guilt-fired imagination.

While coffee was brewing, they turned on the TV. She almost made a remark about missing her TV over the weekend. She could almost hear Ike asking, "Doesn't your grandmother have television?"

They listened to a news broadcast. The Zanardi case was reviewed. She wasn't surprised that the full autopsy report was still being withheld. This was something they could talk about till coffee was ready. She didn't want to launch into the full details of her subterfuge until he'd had a jolt of caffeine to soften the blow.

"Still nothing about the toxic substance the countess drank," she said.

"No, and there won't be, for a while," he replied. "We're

hoping the perpetrator will decide the autopsy didn't pick up the isopropanol and think we're basing the case solely on the absence of nicotine. I guess you figured that out."

The smoke cover, she thought, nodding.

"You're one of the few people outside the department who knows about the isopropanol," he said.

She couldn't resist a slight dig. "And if Dan hadn't told me, I wouldn't know anything about it, either."

"You're still mad at me from the other night, aren't you?" he asked.

"I wasn't mad at you—just disappointed," she replied. He seemed almost apologetic, she thought. She was the one who should be apologizing.

At that moment the aroma of coffee permeated the apartment. She went behind the screen and filled two mugs.

"Liz," he said, when he'd taken a couple of swallows, "I want to explain why I didn't let you in on anything the other night."

She nodded. "I'm listening."

"The DA's been on vacation and I got a tip about one of the attorneys on his staff," Ike said. "Seems this guy's been trying to get a lid put on the kind of good citizen cooperation in homicide cases like we've been involved in. There's a rumor going around he has his eye on the DA's job and he's going to run against him in the primary election."

"I know you have a good working relationship with this DA," Liz said. "You didn't want to do anything to damage him."

"That's it, exactly. This fellow was just waiting for something to jump on so he could blow it up and leak it to the news media while the DA was away."

"Sneaky. Is the DA back yet?"

"He'll be back tomorrow."

"When he gets wind of what this sneak was doing, will he want you to cut me off?"

"No. You've been too helpful. This wannabe DA could

have distorted our cooperation behind the DA's back, but not when he's on the job again."

"I wish you'd told me this before." She almost added, "Before I took matters into my own hands."

"I should have told you about it that night. I was going to tell you the next time I saw you, after I got a firm line on what this guy was up to, but . . ."

"But I told you I was going to Gram's for the weekend, so you had to put it off till now."

"Right," he said. Again, she thought he seemed subdued. After a moment he said, "Now, how about what *you* have to tell *me?*"

She took a deep breath. "Will you promise to hear me out? No interruptions?"

"I promise."

"Okay then. But first I should explain that this never would have happened if I'd known why you wouldn't discuss the Zanardi case with me. I felt so shut out and frustrated. I just had to do some investigating on my own."

She paused to glance at him. His face looked impassive. True to his promise, he made no attempt to speak.

She swallowed hard and took another deep breath. "I didn't spend the weekend with my grandmother—I took a job as a maid in the Hunterdon house so I could get a handle on all the suspects and maybe come up with some clues. I lied to you, Ike. I felt awful about it the whole time. I've never felt so sorry about anything in my life." She didn't dare look at him. "I wouldn't blame you if you walked out the door and never came back."

She still couldn't look at him, but her mind pictured his eyes staring at her, angry, cold and unforgiving. The silence seemed interminable. Anything would be better than this, she thought. "Please, say something," she whispered.

"I knew you weren't with your grandmother," he said.

Now she looked at him, startled. She couldn't define the expression on his face, but one thing she was sure of—it wasn't anger. Maybe he hadn't forgiven her, but at least he hadn't walked out. She breathed a sigh of relief. "How did you know?" she asked.

"I was sitting in my car in Moravian cemetery, Saturday afternoon, observing Countess Zanardi's burial, and I saw your grandmother, also watching the proceedings," he said. "I knew any woman her age able to walk from her house, across Richmond Road and all the way up to the Hunterdon plot had to be in pretty good shape. She certainly didn't need her granddaughter to take care of her all weekend. Then, when I phoned you at her house and she said you were out doing errands for her, I suspected she was covering for you and you'd gone somewhere else for the weekend. And then when you called me back and the caller ID didn't show a name or number, I was pretty sure you weren't, and never had been, at your grandmother's house."

All Liz could say was, "Oh." Hearing her deception described in his own words made her wonder if things would ever be the same between them.

"Then I got thinking," Ike continued. "I figured if your grandmother was hanging around the Hunterdon plot the day of the countess' burial, the two of you must be up to something involving the case."

Liz found her voice. "Did you suspect I was working undercover at the Hunterdon house?"

He cast her a stern look. "Do you think if I did, I wouldn't have gone over there and dragged you out?"

"Would you actually have done that?" she asked, pleased with the idea.

"You're damn right I would. You were living in the same house with the killer!"

She stared at him. He'd as much as said the murderer was a member of the household.

He must have interpreted the stare. "I said that rather loosely. Of course there are other suspects who don't live there," he said.

"Like the count and the linebacker?" she asked.

He flashed a grin. "I guess you have all the suspects

listed in your notebook. How about reading me your notes?"

What are you waiting for? a voice within her urged. *Give him the parcel now.*

But if she did, she'd have to tell him what motivated her to search the storeroom. Ike was too good a detective not to sense something when she mentioned Randolph's presence in the kitchen on Sunday. She'd find herself telling him about the assault. He might be angry. At the very least, he'd bring up all the other predicaments her snooping had gotten her into. With things going along so smoothly between them, she decided not to make waves. She wanted to know more details about the case. She'd put off telling him about the bottle till they'd discussed it some more.

She reached into her purse and brought out her notebook. "I'll read you what I wrote and you can judge for yourself if I picked up anything worthwhile," she said.

She read him everything she'd written, feeling thankful she hadn't described the incident with Randolph. He jotted down some of her notes in his own notebook.

When she finished, he gave a whistle. "I have to hand it to you, Liz, you've got a lot of material there."

"Anything you didn't already know?"

"Sure. Randolph being promised the BMW."

His mention of Randolph jolted her. But she might as well get used to his name coming up frequently. Suddenly she knew keeping the bottle under wraps was going to get more difficult every minute, and she couldn't put it off much longer.

"Anything else?" she asked.

"Yes. The servants opened up to you. They told you things that our interviews didn't fully bring out—like the countess being jealous of her brother and being mean to him when they were kids. Also, we knew the servants weren't fond of the countess, but you found out they both disliked her, intensely. And some of your notes on Miss Jane are helpful too. We're not ruling anyone out, yet."

His last remark, coming right after his mention of Miss Jane, made her think Miss Jane was at the top of his suspect list. As she thought this over, she noticed his coffee mug was empty. "How about a refill?" she asked.

He handed her the mug with a smile, and continued talking after she went behind the kitchenette screen. "Another thing—when we interviewed Fannie we got the impression that she likes Miss Jane, but you found out it goes beyond that. You say Fannie almost idolizes her."

He was thinking Fannie could have had a motive other than her bequest, Liz decided. End the abuse dealt to her adored Miss Jane.

"Was Miss Jane mentioned in the countess' will?" she asked.

"Yes, but the countess didn't leave her any money—just a mink coat."

"I've heard it said some women would kill for a mink coat," Liz joked, returning with the coffee.

He laughed. "Not Miss Jane. In my first interview with her I found out she's an animal rights advocate."

"And of course the countess was totally unaware of that," Liz said, with a wry smile. "Did Gus Stanky get any money?"

"Yes, and the other husband too, and Fannie. And of course the brother got the bulk of the estate. But getting back to Miss Jane—that remark you said Myrtle made about the countess having something on her ties right in with what Lou and I concluded."

"I know *you* came back and questioned her again. Was that why?"

"Yes. I'm still working on that angle." He looked at her with a slight frown. "I have to admit, we haven't made much progress, Maybe we'll get a lead after we sort over what you've come up with."

She glanced at the tote bag. Had she actually come up with something she wondered, or had her wildfire imagination carried her too far? But she hadn't imagined the date on the package. Whether or not Randolph was guilty, the missing bottle had to be in that parcel. She decided to tell Ike, now, that she'd found it. She took a deep breath, but Ike's next words stopped hers.

"We're up against a clever perpetrator," he said. "For example, we found a vodka bottle in the countess' night-stand but lab tests didn't show any isopropanol. Evidently a vodka bottle from the house liquor supply had been put in place of the other one. Unfortunately the killer would have disposed of the contaminated bottle right away. As you know, we haven't released any information about the missing bottle. And because there's been nothing said about isoproponal in a vodka bottle, the murderer assumes we don't know about the substituted bottle."

"So the killer believes the police think the bottle found in the cabinet is the one the countess drank out of," Liz said.

"Right," he replied. He gave a rueful frown. "The original bottle would have been important evidence."

That did it. She reached into her tote bag and took out the package.

"Is that what you said you were going to show me?" he asked.

"Yes. I found it in the Hunterdon's storeroom."

He cast her a quizzical look. "What's in it?"

"I didn't open it," she replied, handing him the parcel. "But from the shape and size, I'm sure there's a bottle in there. I thought *you* should open it."

He laughed. "The missing bottle? What I wouldn't give if it was. But you know as well as I, that bottle's in some landfill by now."

"Take a look at the date on the newspaper."

The instant Ike saw the date his face lit up with excited anticipation. He undid the twine. Slowly, carefully he began to unwrap the package.

Chapter Thirteen

Liz gasped. Ike gave a satisfied grunt. In the folds of the newspaper lay a flat-shaped pint bottle, empty, but bearing a vodka label. She noticed one corner of the label was ragged and loose, suggesting an attempt had been made to remove it.

Ike pulled her into his arms, almost roughly, as if he were too jubilant to be gentle. "Looks like you've done it again, Liz," he said, before they were locked in a kiss.

All her regrets and self-recriminations were swept away in those few moments. "Does this mean you've forgiven me?" she whispered, afterward.

"I forgave you even before I knew where you spent the weekend."

She looked at him in puzzlement. "When?"

"On the phone, when you said you had something serious to tell me. I'd already figured you'd lied to me about spending the weekend with your grandmother, but when you came out with that on the phone I knew you were going to be straight with me." He cast her a teasing smile. "Besides, how could I not forgive you when you've come up with a breakthrough? All we need is for the lab tests to show the bottle contains traces of isopropanol."

Liz loved it when he said "we". It meant they'd be swapping ideas, again. But he hadn't asked her, yet, how she happened to think of searching the storeroom. She hoped he wouldn't think about that any time soon. She knew she'd be in for plenty of teasing about her over-active imagination.

"Another factor," Ike said. "This wasn't considered a homicide till Wednesday night. There was no reason for the perp to get rid of the bottle in a hurry. That makes me ready to eliminate the two ex-husbands as suspects. Either one of them would have taken the bottle with him—but according to household members they both left soon after the countess was put to bed. The timing's off. The killer is someone living in the house."

Her first responding thought was of Randolph. Her next was that Ike had talked a lot about Miss Jane. Did he have strong suspicions about her?

Ike continued, "The way I figure it, the minute the police arrived, the perp knew there'd be a search so he took the bottle out of its hiding place and kept it on his person during the interviews. A flat bottle like that could easily be concealed in an inside pocket of a jacket or the pocket of any bulky garment."

Liz noticed Ike was now referring to the killer as "he". Was this a generality, or was a male member of the household now his prime suspect? She pictured Randolph, wearing a British hacking jacket, being questioned by detectives, watching the uniforms go over every inch of the house and yard, while the bottle was nestled in one of his pockets. But of course the same could be true of Miss Jane. She often wore a jacket. The other women in the house didn't.

But Ike had started her thinking of the killer as male. "And then when the police left, he hid the bottle somewhere in the house, again, and planned to take it out of the house as soon as he got the chance," she said.

Randolph might not have had the chance to do it, but she mustn't forget the others, male or not. Any one of them could have taken the bottle out of house as soon as the police left. Well, maybe not Myrtle or Fannie; they were generally confined to the premises except on their days off. She tried to figure out if they'd had a day off since the murder, but she couldn't make a positive determination.

"You finding the bottle in the house puts another slant on the case," Ike said. "With nothing in the news about isoproponal in the bottle, it's possible the killer decided he'd gotten away with it. And since he was in no hurry, he wrapped the bottle in the newspaper and waited for the opportune time to get it out of the house."

"But before he wrapped it in the newspaper, it must have been wrapped in something else," she said.

"Right. He wouldn't have hidden it without concealing it in something. An article of clothing, maybe."

Liz imagined the bottle being wrapped in a shirt or sweater and stashed in a dresser drawer. "I guess any lint on the bottle could be picked up at the police lab and cross tested with the suspects' clothing," she said.

She pictured the dresser drawers of all the Hunterdon males being emptied and the contents borne off to the police lab. But she shouldn't forget that the bottle could have been wrapped in clothing belonging to Miss Jane, or the other female members of the household.

"That's going to be a long, slow procedure," she said.

As she spoke, a sudden, unexpected feeling struck her. Maybe it was because his arms hadn't fully released her from their last hug. She wanted to take a break from the case. She'd never felt like this before. Nothing had ever taken priority over the homicide case she was into. But then, till recently, Ike hadn't been a strong presence in her life.

She knew he'd sensed something when he looked straight into her eyes and asked, "What's on your mind?"

"Could we knock off talking about the Zanardi case for a while?"

He gave a hearty laugh. "I never thought I'd hear you say anything like that."

"It was kind of a surprise to me too."

"Well, you've never done three days of non-stop snooping before. You'll be back to normal tomorrow," he said. His arms, still holding her loosely, now tightened around her. "Meanwhile, we'd better take advantage of this unusual situation."

Though he spoke lightly, almost jokingly, she saw no humor in his eyes—only a look that told her his feelings were as strong as hers. All her thoughts and fantasies of the past few weeks sprang alive at that moment.

They were coming out of a kiss when her phone rang.

"Do you have to answer that?" he asked.

She checked the caller ID. "It's Gram," she said. "I told her I'd be home tonight. I'd better pick up or she'll worry."

Gram's voice broke the spell she'd been under—the spell of being in Ike's arms and knowing he was as deeply mesmerized as she. "I hope I'm not calling too late, dear. Are you in bed yet?"

"Not quite." Liz couldn't hold back a laugh.

Ike gave a questioning look that seemed to ask, "What's so funny?" When she told him, he'd laugh too, she thought. Seeing humor in the same things was almost as important as the feelings they'd shared, moments ago.

"I just wanted to make sure you were home safe and sound," Gram said.

No matter what, I'll always be safe and sound with Ike.

"Thanks for checking up on me, Gram," she replied. "I got home a little while ago and I'm fine."

After she and Gram said good-bye, she noticed Ike looking at the bottle, not touching it, but giving it a thorough optical examination. She knew he'd come out of the spell too.

"I guess you're itching to get the bottle to the lab," she said.

He nodded. "I should run it over there now." Before he got to his feet, he leaned over and gave her a quick kiss.

"I'll drop in tomorrow night and let you know what they picked up."

"There's still a lot we haven't covered," she said.

He nodded. "I know. We'll get to it tomorrow. Thanks for your help, Liz. I don't like the way you accomplished this, but I suppose the end justifies the means."

"I promise I'll never do anything like this again," she said, as they walked to the door.

A slight frown crossed his face, followed by a wry smile. "You won't repeat this exactly, but I know there'll always be something."

She knew he was harking back to the other predicaments her sleuthing had gotten her into. But being held against her will in the apartment of a deranged woman, being followed home and threatened by a murder suspect and especially, being kidnapped by two members of an organized crime family, were dangerous situations. During her three days in the Hunterdon home she hadn't been in any danger.

Then she remembered randy Randolph. She hadn't planned to keep the assault a secret from Ike, indefinitely. Now that she knew everything was all right between them, she might as well tell him about it, now.

At the door, Ike leaned down to kiss her goodnight. Something in her eyes must have alerted him. He stopped short. "What?" he asked.

"I forgot to tell you something," she said, "It can't wait till tomorrow night."

He flashed her a grin. "Should I be sitting down for this?"

Maybe he should, she thought. "No. I know you want to get going. I'll make it quick."

She told him everything, skipping only a few minor details, trying to make light of it. It took only a few minutes.

"It wasn't as bad as it sounds," she said. "Even if Sophie and Mike hadn't shown up, I . . ."

"It sounds bad enough," Ike growled. He put his arms around her and held her close for a few moments, in silence. "It's a good thing I didn't know where you were," he said. "I might have figured young Randolph would hit on a housemaid as pretty as you, and I had enough worries about you after I found out you were spending the weekend with someone other than your grandmother."

"Why were you worried about me?"

"I thought that guy from Philadelphia might be back in the picture."

He was referring to Phil Perillo. Handsome, wealthy, debonair, half-Irish, half-Italian Phil, who chose to play up his Irish half with the most outrageous blarney she'd ever heard. He should have been the man of her dreams, but their relationship ended before it actually began. Ike didn't know it, but *he* was the main reason. Some day she'd let him know.

"What kind of a person do you think I am?" she asked, pretending he'd set off the redhead Irish temper he was always teasing her about. "Do you really think I'd pull something like that?"

"I was jealous," he said. Then, as if the words had slipped out inadvertently, he gave her a quick hug, opened the door and started down the stairs, calling, "I'll see you tomorrow night. I'll phone you at your office and let you know what time."

Jealous! This was the closest he'd come to telling her he didn't want her seeing any other man. And not wanting her to see any other man could mean the L word might be as near as tomorrow.

Chapter Fourteen

The next morning Sophie phoned her at the office. "I knew you were home last night and I was going to call you," she said. "But then I decided Ike would be there. I didn't want to interrupt anything."

Sophie was hellbent for a romance between her best friend and the former Detective Sourpuss, Liz thought. She must remember to tell Sophie about Gram's laugh-provoking phone call. "When are we going to get together?" she asked.

"How about after work today at the coffee shop near the station house?" Sophie replied. "I'm meeting Ralph for dinner, but not till six-thirty."

"That'll be good. Ike said he'd phone me about coming over tonight. I'll tell him to make it after six-thirty."

How suddenly things had changed, Liz thought, as she hung up the phone. Only a couple of months ago she and Sophie met almost every day after work for coffee and often for dinner and a movie. They used to exchange confidences about the men they were seeing—brief relationships which hadn't made it into commitments, but mostly they'd discuss the sensational homicide case currently rocking Manhattan.

In a city where drug and gang-related killings were common occurrences, occasionally there'd be a murder case involving the rich and famous that captured newspaper headlines and intensive TV coverage. Sophie used to be into these kinds of cases almost as much as she. They both loved delving into them, piecing together her own information from Dan with what Sophie picked up when she was in the squad room, plus what they got from the news media.

Now Sophie was a patrol cop, soon to be married to another cop. Though she still enjoyed following murder cases, her life was beginning to revolve around Ralph and their wedding, planned for October.

And my own life? Following sensational homicides remained her passion; perhaps more than ever since Ike had become her prime source of information.

But that wasn't all he'd become. Once they'd gotten past the hostile stage, their relationship had settled into the tranquility of a placid pond. But within the past few weeks, it had become a stream of fast-flowing water building up behind a weakening dam. Abruptly, she thrust the disturbing metaphor out of her mind with a firm resolution. She would not allow herself to be swept away till Ike made his feelings a lot clearer than he had, so far.

Actions were supposed to speak louder than words, but as much as she enjoyed the action, she wanted to hear the words.

In the coffee shop, Sophie fired a barrage of questions without waiting for answers. Had Liz picked up any clues? Had she honed in on a prime suspect? Had she told Ike about her undercover operation? How did he react?

"I'll answer all your questions in the order of their importance," Liz said with a laugh. "Yes, I came clean with Ike and his reaction surprised me. He wasn't mad." She told Sophie how Ike had seen Gram in the cemetery and put two and two together.

"One of the hazards of dating a detective—you can't get

away with anything much," Sophie said. She paused, stirring her coffee.

"I know you're thinking Ike wasn't mad because I came up with some clues for him," Liz said. She realized Sophie didn't know about the coma-inducing substance in the vodka bottle—information strictly guarded in Dan's office. Though she couldn't let Sophie in on this, she could tell her what she'd picked up while she was Beth the chambermaid.

"So, what did you find out?" Sophie asked.

Liz went down the list, starting with the root of it all, the countess' hateful disposition. She wanted to include everything except the matter of the incomplete autopsy report.

She started to tell her about finding the bottle, but Sophie broke in. "Wow!" she said, "everyone had a motive. Who's at the top of your list?"

Liz took a swallow of coffee. "Wait till you hear this," she replied. She told Sophie the whole story about Randolph and how she found the bottle.

"You found the bottle! That's great!" The next moment, Sophie looked dubious. "But I don't buy the idea of the kid hiding it in the storeroom. He hadn't lived in the house long enough to be familiar with the layout. How would he even know there *was* a storeroom in the kitchen area? And I can't imagine that bumbling kid planning the murder."

Liz had to agree this made sense.

"What does Ike think about it?" Sophie asked.

"I didn't get around to telling him I suspect Randolph, and why."

"Didn't he want to know why you decided to search the storeroom?"

"No, he didn't." She remembered those moments before Gram's phone call. He'd been too distracted, she decided.

"Oh, I get it," Sophie said, looking pleased. "You didn't spend the entire evening talking about the case. But sooner or later Ike's going to ask how come you thought the bottle might be hidden in the storeroom."

"I know, and I'm not looking forward to telling him."

"Why not?"

"I'll be in for an awful teasing."

"Guys like to tease gals they're in love with," Sophie said. "Any developments in that area?"

Liz thought of Ike's parting words last night: *I was jealous.* "Maybe a little," she replied.

"But at least he's been letting you in on the angles of the case, hasn't he?"

"Sure, but there's something he's clammed up about—his investigation of Miss Jane."

"He's been looking into her past?"

"Yes, but he hasn't told me what he dug up, if anything."

"Her relationship with the countess is like a mystery within a mystery," Sophie said. "It suggests blackmail. That would be a pretty strong motive for murder."

Liz nodded. "I know, but I can't imagine Miss Jane killing anyone for any reason."

Sophie looked thoughtful. "You say nobody in the household believes it was homicide?"

"That's right," Liz replied. "They all insist the countess fell asleep smoking in bed. Knowing she always went to bed smashed, I'd go along with that myself, but no nicotine showed up in the autopsy."

"With the autopsy showing she hadn't been smoking, you'd think they'd accept the fact that someone planted the lit cigarette in her carpet," Sophie said. "Looks to me like the killer sold this accidental death idea to the rest of the household."

"I think so too."

"You say the brother's trying to get the homicide judgement reversed. Could he have been the one who started everyone believing it wasn't homicide?"

"It looks like he'd be the logical one," Liz replied. "But

if he was, maybe this didn't have anything to do with the
actual murder. Maybe he only wanted to remove the stigma
of murder from his family name."

She paused to take a drink of her coffee. "Ike and I didn't
half cover everything last night. I hope after we toss some
ideas around tonight, we can come up with some conclu-
sions."

"The angle about the kid and the BMW is interesting,"
Sophie said. "Did you tell Ike about the assault?"

"Yes. I was afraid he'd hear about it somehow."

"How did he take it? Did he blow his top?"

"No. He took it with amazing cool. I got the impression
he's resigned to me getting into predicaments."

"That's surprising for a guy in love," Sophie said. "And
don't try and tell me he isn't."

Liz shook her head. "If he is, he hasn't said anything."

"Ralph didn't mention love for a long time, either. I finally had to give it a shove."

"You mean, you said it first?"

"Not exactly. I just said enough to give him the idea.
You should try that tactic." Sophie checked her watch. "We
better finish our coffee. It's time we got going."

"Thanks for the advice," Liz said, as they left the coffee
shop. "I'm not saying I have the nerve to follow it though."

First things first, she thought, as she walked to the subway. With Ike's mind squarely on the Zanardi case, this
was no time for trying to sneak in other ideas.

Shortly after she got home, Ike arrived with Chinese
takeout and a bottle of white Zinfandel.

"Do you mind eating in tonight?" he asked.

"Of course not." He wanted more talk time, she decided.

While he helped her set up the gateleg table, she noticed
he seemed weary. His face looked tired, too, as if he hadn't
been getting much sleep lately. He and Lou must be putting
in a lot of overtime on this case. He might be discouraged

too. Until the bottle showed up, there hadn't been prospects of a significant breakthrough.

"Here, we can talk freely about the case," he said.

That pretty well summed up what was foremost on his mind, Liz thought, with a wry smile.

"Don't bother switching from the cartons into serving dishes," Ike said, resting the sack of takeout on the gateleg table. "Let's just dig it out of the boxes onto our plates."

"Okay with me," Liz replied. They unpacked the cartons and sat down. Ike poured the wine.

"Here's to a quick solution to the case," she said, raising her glass.

He smiled as they touched goblets. "We got the test results on the vodka bottle."

"What came up?"

"The bottle had been emptied and rinsed, but there was still clear evidence of isopropanol."

"I guess that firmly establishes the bottle as the one the countess drank out of."

"Right."

"Any prints on it?"

"Nothing that could be lifted. And the same goes for the newspaper wrapping. Our prints blurred any the perp might have left." He paused to bite into his egg roll.

"Didn't anything else show up on the bottle—like lint from whatever it was wrapped in?"

"Yeah, the torn label got wet when the killer rinsed the bottle and the dry glue got sticky. There was lint on it, and a trace of hair. It'll take time to test articles the bottle might have been wrapped in, but when there's a match with what's on the bottle, we'll have our killer."

"But wouldn't a DNA test on all the suspects' hair be enough?" she asked. "You could get it from their combs and brushes."

He shook his head. "We also need a match on the lint texture and the bits of gluey paper. Combs and brushes can be interchanged."

At first Liz couldn't picture Hunterdon household members using one another's combs and brushes. On second thought, she supposed it could happen with David and Randolph.

She considered suggesting that hair could be taken directly from suspects' heads, but there had to be a reason why Ike hadn't mentioned that. Maybe Ike and Lou didn't want their strategy spelled out. Taking hair samples from everyone in the household might tip the killer off.

Ike dipped a spoon into one of the takeout cartons. "Are you ready for some of this General Tsao's chicken?"

"Yes, please. And whatever's in the other boxes too. I'm hungry."

"General Tsao, Shrimp Lo Mein and Moo Shu coming right up," he said. He spooned portions of the spicy chicken, the shrimp and the Chinese noodles and vegetables onto their plates and added some rice.

"So what next?" she asked.

He flashed her a grin. "I guess you're entitled to know what I've been up to today. Among other things, I've been making inquiries into Alistair Hunterdon's financial status."

"Didn't you do that already, to find out if he came back to New York because he was broke?"

"Sure. And we found out he's not broke. According to the New York banks, he's in great shape, and going into a business partnership with another multi-millionaire, putting up a luxury condo tower. But we wanted to dig deeper to make sure money couldn't have been a motive. I've been on the phone and the Internet with London."

"And . . . ?"

"He's in excellent financial shape, and besides that, Lady Sylvia is independently wealthy."

"So you're striking the need for money as his motive."

"Right. And we believe the ill feeling between Alistair and his sister doesn't stack up as strong enough."

"Are you saying Alistair's off the suspect list?"

"Let's just say he's the low man."

"And Lady Sylvia?"

"She's right down there with him, along with David."

"But not Randolph?"

A slight frown crossed Ike's face. "No, not Randolph."

"Because of the BMW?"

"That's a factor, but you should know there's another reason."

"You're talking about him coming on to me."

"Damn right—and you shouldn't dismiss it so lightly. When you told me what happened, it looked to me like the kid has a violent streak."

She held back the urge to remind him that he hadn't been at the scene or he would have realized that Randolph's anger had been more like a childish tantrum. Sure it had scared her for a few minutes, but it was nowhere near violence.

"I felt strongly enough about it to contact Scotland Yard to see if he had a record," Ike said. "I thought maybe that was the reason his father moved the family to New York. He wanted to get his son out of London."

Liz recalled Pop telling her more than once that Ike was a super detective. Checking out Randolph with Scotland Yard proved it, she thought. Then the idea of bungling, adolescent Randolph having a criminal record struck her as amusing. "So, did you find out he's another Jack the Ripper?" she asked.

The suggestion of a smile warmed the serious look on Ike's face. "Not even close," he said. "As far as Scotland Yard's concerned, the kid's as clean as a whistle. But there's still the matter of the BMW. He's still a strong suspect."

Would knowing about Randolph's presence in the countess' bedroom and in the kitchen near the storeroom strengthen his suspicions? She thought of telling him now how she happened to search the storeroom, but she wanted to return to the subject of the bottle.

"Getting back to the lint on the bottle, how are you going

to decide what it might have been wrapped in and what to test?"

"The tests narrowed down the fabric to cotton, and the lint was coarse enough to rule out certain lighter articles like pillowcases or shirts."

"Or underwear, or a maid's uniform or apron?"

Ike nodded. "It had to be something with a heavier texture, something knitted, maybe."

"Could it have been a cotton blanket or a Turkish towel, or maybe a cotton knit sweater?"

"A blanket, yeah, or a sweater, but we hope it wasn't a towel. A towel would have gone through the washer and dryer by now."

Liz nodded. A towel would have been returned to the linen closet by this time with the evidence washed away. But would the killer have wrapped the bottle in something as large as a blanket? Maybe it was more like a throw. Come to think of it, she'd noticed a white knitted-throw draped across the chaise in the Hunterdons' bedroom.

Two provocative thoughts struck her. Maybe Fannie or Myrtle had a cotton knit throw, and either one of them could have hidden the bottle in the storeroom, intending to take it out of the house on her day off. Her thoughts returned to the residue on the bottle.

"What color was the lint?" she asked.

"White. Did you notice anyone at the Hunterdons' wearing a white cotton sweater? Either a man or a woman?"

"I don't recall," Liz replied. "But of course while I was there I wasn't alert for white cotton sweaters."

"The men would be more likely to have one," Ike said. "Lady Sylvia doesn't strike me as someone who'd wear something so informal. She might have a knit scarf or shawl though. The lint could be from something like that."

"Or a knit throw," Liz replied. She told him about seeing one on Lady Sylvia's chaise. "I guess Fannie and Myrtle might have something like that too," she added. "But not that sporty kind of sweater."

But she'd noticed Miss Jane favored casual clothing. In a flash of recollection, she realized Miss Jane had on a white cotton knit sweater the day of the job interview.

Ike must have noticed Miss Jane's taste in clothes. Maybe he'd seen her in her white sweater, but he wasn't ready to mention it, any more than he was ready to divulge what he'd found out about Miss Jane's past—if anything. For some reason he was keeping his thoughts concerning Miss Jane to himself.

She decided not to mention Miss Jane's sweater. Ike wouldn't overlook it when possible evidence was collected for testing.

With a satisfied smile, Ike rested his fork on his plate. "I'm full."

"Me too," she replied. "There's a lot left over. Do you want to take some home with you?"

"Sure, but does that mean you're easing me out the door?"

"Of course not. You know I'd never send you home without dessert and coffee. I have chocolate ice cream and some cookies Rosa brought up."

Since Ike had been coming over regularly, Rosa had been dropping in with samples of her baking. Store-bought cake and cookies were as unfit for "that nice young cop" as pasta sauce in a jar and cheese in a carton.

"When are you going to start looking for things like white shawls and sweaters?" she asked, while they were drinking their after-dinner coffee.

"We have a search warrant for tomorrow morning."

She got the feeling this was as much as she'd hear about the case tonight. Now might be an opportune time to try out Sophie's tactics. Ralph had been silent on the subject of love, she'd said. She had to give it a shove.

Okay, Liz thought, I can do that.

"Thanks for being concerned about my unpleasant encounter with Randolph," she said.

"It was a hell of a lot more than just concern."

She took a deep breath. "Why?"

He cast her a long look over their empty ice cream bowls and the half-full boxes of Chinese takeout. "Surely you know how I feel about you, Liz."

"Not really."

He reached across the table and took her hands. For a moment the cliché, *my heart stood still*, wasn't a cliché at all. And at that moment his phone rang.

Chapter Fifteen

Her previous assumption had been right, Liz thought. Ike and Lou had been working overtime on this case. Now Lou was calling with something important.

She suppressed a sigh. It *better* be important. At the rate they were progressing, Ike would never get around to telling her what she wanted to hear.

She listened to Ike's cryptic questions and comments on the phone. "Right" . . . "Yeah?" . . . "Tonight?" . . . "Good" . . . "Okay, I'm on my way."

With a rueful smile, he shoved the phone back into his pocket and got to his feet. "Sorry, I have to pull an eat-and-run."

She rose from her chair, feeling disappointed. It looked as if her assumption that Ike and Lou were working overtime wasn't the only thing she'd been right about. It sounded like Ike had information he hadn't let her in on. As a homicide detective's daughter, she should understand and be satisfied with what he'd already told her. She *was* satisfied, to a degree. But she'd come up with the vodka bottle. He'd told her finding it was a breakthrough. Didn't she deserve to know what new information he had?

Maybe if she questioned him, he'd reconsider and at least

give her a hint. "Did Lou uncover something important?" she asked, as they started towards the door.

"I was just going to tell you that wasn't Lou on the phone," he replied. "I'll give you the details tomorrow night."

How quickly those few words changed her mood from glum to gleeful. But they also heightened her curiosity. If that wasn't Lou on the phone, who was it? "Can't you fill me in now?" she asked.

She saw indecision in his eyes. "I haven't got enough yet. If I told you what little I have, you'd be awake all night. Wouldn't you rather wait? I'm meeting someone who's going to give me vital information."

"I'll be awake all night if you *don't* tell what you have now."

He hesitated for a moment before replying. "Well, all right. I already told you I've been checking Miss Jane's background . . ."

Her mind tingled with anticipation. "You've picked up something about her husband's murder?"

"I won't know for sure till I've met with the person who phoned me." He paused, as if to give her time to change her mind and say she'd wait till he had more information.

She held back an impatient sigh. "If you knew how much time I've spent puzzling about Miss Jane, you'd realize how much I want to know *anything*."

"All right," he said. "I've connected with someone who has information about a nine-year-old cold case. I have a hunch it might be the murder of Miss Jane's husband."

Liz's reaction was instantaneous. *Could Miss Jane have been implicated?*

She didn't know exactly how this registered on her face, but however it did, it made him laugh. "I told you it would be best to wait till I got the full story," he said.

He was right. This was like being given a drop of water when you were dying of thirst.

"I'd suggest coming back later tonight to let you know

what I find out, but I don't know how long this meeting's going to run," he said.

She understood. It could run late, and he wanted to get enough sleep so he'd be alert tomorrow morning. The search for possible evidence at the Hunterdon home would require a lot of mental energy.

"Good luck tomorrow," she said. "Where are you going to start first?"

"Members of the evidence crew will work simultaneously in each area," he replied. "That way there'll be less chance of tipping our hand to the killer."

He thought the killer might guess what the search was all about and attempt to foul things up, she decided. "You'll have to keep your eye on everyone," she said. Especially Miss Jane, she thought. If she was involved in her husband's death, she might also be capable of planning the countess' murder.

"I wish we could herd all the suspects into one room and lock the door while the search is underway," Ike replied. "But we'll manage."

"Well, I know you want to get going. Thanks for telling me about your meeting tonight. You can't imagine how I feel when you shut me out. You can't always tell me everything—I know that, but I hope you'll continue letting me know as much as you can."

As she spoke, she looked into his eyes. For an instant she saw a flicker of expression she could not define. "See you tomorrow night," he said, after giving her a kiss and a hug.

She sensed he'd been about to say something else.

She cleared away the remains of their dinner, her mind teeming with questions. What had Ike almost said, and why hadn't he said it? Did it have anything to do with the person Ike was meeting? Was this person a regular police informant? If he knew something about the shooting death of Miss Jane's husband, why hadn't he told the police at the time of the murder, nine years ago? Did Miss Jane know this person? Could there have been a connection between this informant and the countess?

She couldn't come up with any answers that made sense. By the time she got into her pajamas and opened her sofa bed, her mind was exhausted from speculation. She was ready to think about something else. Sliding under Gram's patchwork quilt, she switched off the light and turned her thoughts to tomorrow's search at the Hunterdon house.

Even with the evidence crew working in different areas at the same time, the search would be tedious, she thought. All those dresser drawers and closets to go through, looking for something the bottle could have been wrapped in.

Again she hoped the evidence crew would keep alert to the behavior of all household members. Even though the killer didn't know the police were wise to the isoproponal in the bottle, and even though he didn't know the bottle had been found and tested, when he saw what the police were doing he'd have to be pretty dense not to put two and two together. Again she was concerned that if he figured it all out, he might do something to sabotage the procedure.

She was growing sleepy when she realized she was still making mental reference to the killer as male. In light of possible new evidence against Miss Jane, she should get over that. A dream-like picture formed in her mind of Miss Jane being nice and cooperative towards the police crew, offering the sweater she was wearing for testing, and then going into a bathroom other than her own to change, and contaminating her sweater with hair from someone else's brush or comb.

Did Ike have the same idea she asked herself drowsily. Is that what he'd almost said? The question had almost faded into sleep when her phone rang. Instantly she came out of her languor and answered.

Ike's voice tore away the fringes of sleep. "Liz, I'm sorry if I woke you up. I just got home and there's something I want to tell you."

She knew he wouldn't discuss tonight's meeting over the phone. He must be calling about something else. "I wasn't asleep yet," she said. "What's up?"

"I've been working on another angle," he said. "Nothing to do with Miss Jane. It's a long shot and I don't expect anything to come of it, but I thought you might enjoy speculating about it."

This must be what he'd almost told her before he left tonight, she decided. She'd probably made him feel guilty when she said she hoped he'd continue to let her in on whatever he could.

"Well, thanks," she said. "But before you tell me about this long shot, how'd your meeting go tonight?"

"Very well. You know I can't talk about it on the phone, but I promise to give you a full report when I see you tomorrow night."

"But you can talk on the phone about the long shot?"

"I can give you something to play around with. Maybe it will get your mind off Miss Jane till I see you tomorrow night."

"That's very thoughtful of you, Detective. So let's hear it."

"Okay. When I was in touch with Scotland Yard about Randolph, I thought as long as I had the contact I might as well have them run a check on another Brit—Myrtle."

"Myrtle? You weren't kidding when you said it was a long shot."

"Yeah. The initial check showed no criminal record, but she was among those questioned in connection with a death in the London house where she was working—an old case Scotland Yard first considered a homicide."

"*First considered a homicide?* What does that mean?"

"Evidently there was some controversy at the time. But getting back to Myrtle, Scotland Yard's still digging for me but I don't expect they'll find anything. There's been nothing questionable about her since she came over here. No immigration irregularities or anything else. But I thought as long as I was in touch with Scotland Yard I'd have them run an intensive check. Well, I better hang up and let you get to sleep."

"Thanks for calling," she said. "See you tomorrow."

She turned out her light, thinking he was wrong if he believed his little surprise regarding Myrtle would take her mind off Miss Jane. The idea of an informant knowing something about the murder of Miss Jane's husband stirred her imagination. Pop had told her about prison informants. It had been nine years since Miss Jane's husband was gunned down. The case was never solved. What if whoever killed him had served time for an unrelated crime since then? And what if his and Ike's informant knew each other in prison? There was no telling what Ike could have found out tonight.

She was getting drowsy when she thought, again, about tomorrow's evidence search. Instantly, she was wide awake. What if none of the things taken to the police lab provided a match with what was on the bottle? That could mean Ike's misgivings had materialized—the vodka bottle had been wrapped in a towel. It had been re-wrapped in the newspaper and the towel sent to the laundry room. It would have been washed by now.

Was there a chance the gluey bits of paper from the torn label on the bottle could have withstood the washing? Would there still be traces of it on the towel in question? Maybe—but what a tremendous job it would be to test every towel in the house.

At that moment a sudden flash of memory lit up her mind. The laundry room came into focus, and the basket of soiled articles she'd talked Fannie into leaving unwashed for a few days. *Myrtle's things*, including her bath towel with the identifying green stripe at the bottom edge.

She turned on her lamp, grabbed her phone and called Ike. "Now it's my turn to say sorry if I woke you up," she said.

"I know you wouldn't be calling if it wasn't important," he replied. "What's going on?"

"Before you organize the evidence search at the Hunterdon house tomorrow, please check with Fannie to find out if she washed Myrtle's things yet."

"Do you mind running that by me again?"

"Fannie was annoyed with Myrtle and she held off washing Myrtle's things when she was doing the laundry on Monday. She said she wasn't going to wash any more of her stuff for a few days. It's in a basket on the floor of the laundry room, at least it was there when I left, and more has probably accumulated. You might have to dig to find the towel."

"Towel?"

"Yes. Myrtle gave it to Fannie to wash on Monday, along with a bunch of other things. It's a white towel with a green border. There might be a couple more towels like it in the basket by now. Be sure you get the one down near the bottom."

"Let me get this straight. You think the bottle was wrapped in one of Myrtle's towels?"

Liz felt foolish all of a sudden. "I just thought it should be tested before you go to all the trouble of searching for sweaters and things."

"All right. We'll do that." His voice sounded more placating than impressed.

She wished she hadn't called him. "I guess I let my imagination run loose after you told me about Scotland Yard and Myrtle," she said. Just as it had when she suspected Randolph, she thought. "But I know you've been hoping the bottle hadn't been wrapped in a towel because all the towels would have been washed. When I remembered Myrtle's unwashed towel, I thought I'd latched onto something hot."

"This wouldn't be the first time you came up with a hot clue," he said.

Her self-confidence came back in a rush. "Then you'll look for the towel first, before you do anything else?"

"Right."

"And have it tested?"

"I will."

She gave a sigh of satisfaction. "Thanks. We'd both better get some sleep now."

She lay awake for quite a while after they said good-bye. Myrtle's towel had made her a prime suspect, but Miss Jane was still right up there. Randolph was all but off her list. Sleep couldn't take over while she tried to decide if either Myrtle or Miss Jane could have murdered the countess. She kept alternating between doubt that either of them was the killer, and being sure one of them was.

When she finally drifted off it was with the thought that even in light of these new developments, it was too soon to label anyone guilty.

Chapter Sixteen

Liz woke the next morning with a strong sense of anticipation. While she showered, while she dressed, while she made coffee and toasted a bagel, thoughts of last night's developments swirled in her mind.

Going to work on the subway, the thoughts changed into questions. Was it possible Miss Jane was not the saintly soul she appeared to be? Would test results on Myrtle's towel show residue that matched what was on the vodka bottle?

On her way to her workstation she passed Dan's office. His door was open and he was at his desk. Except for a few words, they hadn't had a talk since she returned to work after the holiday weekend. She wondered if he knew about Alistair Hunterdon's attempts to have the countess' murder declared an accidental death.

She paused at the door. "Good morning, Dan."

He looked up. "Good morning to you, too, Lizzie. Come on in and let's get caught up before we both get too busy."

It was so great having a boss like Dan, she thought. She debated whether or not to tell him how she'd spent the holiday weekend. There wasn't time to go into that this morning, she decided. Instead she brought up the subject of Alistair's move to have the countess' death declared accidental.

"I guess Eichle told you about that," Dan said. "Yes, Alistair Hunterdon has the whole family believing the postmortem was fouled up."

Not only the family, but the entire household, Liz thought.

"He's trying to convince the DA the medical examiner has a bunch of nincompoops on staff," Dan went on.

"Alistair's going to feel like a fool when it comes out that his sister had isoproponal in her system."

Dan nodded. "I guess Eichle told you the department isn't releasing that information for a while."

"Yes, he did."

"I know you're having a great time with this case, Lizzie. Has Eichle been letting you in on how the investigation's going?"

"He's loosening up more than he used to. But I wouldn't have known about the isoproponal if you hadn't told me."

Dan smiled. "I've known you a lot longer than he has."

She smiled in appreciation. "With that compliment to make my day, I'd better get to work," she said.

She'd been at her desk for about an hour when her phone rang. It was Ike. She caught her breath. "Are you all through at the Hunterdons'?"

"Right. I just wanted to tell you the towel's on its way to the lab."

"Oh, that's great, Ike. Thanks."

"I'll phone you later," he said. He paused. "I guess with all this about the towel, you're not interested anymore in my meeting with the informant."

"Sure I'm still interested," she said. "You know I want to hear anything involving Miss Jane. You better not be backing out."

He laughed. "Hold onto your Irish temper. I'll tell you all about it when I see you tonight. I'm not sure what time

I can get over to your place. I'll phone you and let you know."

He was working overtime on this, she thought. It was surprising he had time for *her*.

For the rest of the morning she was too busy at the computer to concentrate on the new developments in this baffling homicide. When it was time for her lunch break she decided to order in. While eating, she could review the case without distractions. With a BLT on whole wheat, a chocolate cupcake and a container of coffee delivered to her desk, she turned the case over in her mind, first focusing on Myrtle.

Evidently the fact that Myrtle had been among those questioned after a death in the London household where she worked hadn't elevated her to the top of Ike's suspect list. But, like any good detective, he'd been leaving no stone unturned. Scotland Yard was still digging, he'd said, but he didn't expect anything to turn up.

Her idea about Myrtle's towel had changed all that, she thought. The towel was on its way to the police lab. Ike considered it possible evidence. After tests were run, Myrtle could be his prime suspect.

But almost everyone in the household had more reason than Myrtle to want the countess out of the way, she thought, slathering mayo on her sandwich. Myrtle's sole motive would have been her intense dislike of the countess. Would that have been enough to make her commit murder?

It would be helpful if she knew more about Myrtle's background, she thought, taking a swallow of coffee. She knew little about it—only that she'd left London's royal kitchens and come to New York to care for a sick sister, and that she'd worked in a restaurant here.

In order to get the job with the Hunterdons, Myrtle had to provide a recent reference. Evidently the restaurant had given her a good one.

While eating her sandwich, she thought about all the titled families Myrtle had worked for. Myrtle wouldn't have missed the chance to brag about the nobility for whom she'd cooked. No doubt she'd given their names as references. She'd probably even thrown in the Prince of Wales, Liz thought, with a smile.

And Scotland Yard had nothing on Myrtle except a questioning in a long-ago case that wasn't even recorded as a homicide.

These reflections made her wonder if she'd been too hasty in letting Ike know about Myrtle's unwashed towel. Was her desire for his approval so strong that it had clouded her judgement? With a frown, she took the final bite of her sandwich and turned her thoughts to Miss Jane.

Sophie was right when she said the puzzle surrounding Miss Jane was like a mystery within a mystery.

With speculation about Ike's meeting with the informant running rampant in her mind, she started to eat her chocolate cupcake. She loved chocolate, but now she was too deep in thought to enjoy it. She packed most of it into the trash bag with her sandwich wrapper.

Suppose the informant knew that it wasn't an unknown gunman who'd killed Miss Jane's husband, but Miss Jane herself. Suppose the countess had found out, somehow, and held this secret over Miss Jane's head for nine years, keeping her in virtual bondage. What if Miss Jane wanted to break away and marry Gus Stanky and the countess had threatened to reveal the secret?

She swirled her remaining coffee around in the container, staring at it, as if this would unravel the tangled skein of her thoughts. If *she* were able to come to this conclusion about Miss Jane, then Ike had certainly figured it out.

Questions gnawed at her mind. With so much pointing to Miss Jane, why did Ike go along with her brainstorm about Myrtle's towel? Why did he agree to have it tested? Had he done this just to humor her?

She told herself that Ike was too good a detective—too much of a pro to waste department time and money humoring her. Maybe he hadn't sent the towel to the lab at all and planned to tell her the tests were negative. She shook her head. Ike might humor her, but he wouldn't lie to her.

But this was scant comfort. Even if he thought her idea about Myrtle's towel was crazy, they knew one another well enough now for him to be frank with her. All he needed to say was, "That idea doesn't fly."

What was it he'd said when he phoned her about the towel? She searched her mind and recalled: *"The towel's on its way to the lab."* He hadn't said anything about running tests on it and postponing the clothing search at the Hunterdon house. But if it was sent to the lab, of course it would be tested, wouldn't it?

How could she prove to herself that Ike wasn't humoring her? By finding out if the big clothing search at the Hunterdon house had been postponed, that's how. She'd phone the Hunterdon house. She'd identify herself and tell whoever answered that she thought she might have left something in her room—her barrette she'd say. She'd ask whoever answered to please check to see if it was there. She'd say it would be in the top right hand dresser drawer.

In a house like the Hunterdons', the phone most likely would be answered by one of the servants, or maybe Miss Jane. It was almost 1 o'clock. Lunch would be over and the servants would be in the kitchen. If the big search had taken place this morning, she hoped whoever answered the phone would mention it. Otherwise she'd have to ask questions.

Depending on who answered the phone, she could ask if there was anything new concerning the countess' death—things like that. Somehow, she'd find out if the evidence crew had searched the wardrobes of everyone in the house or just taken a towel out of the laundry room.

She looked up the Hunterdons' number in the phone book and placed the call.

"Hunterdon residence." She recognized Fannie's voice.

"Fannie? It's me, Li—uh, Beth."

"Beth!" Fannie sounded as if she were glad to hear from her. "Me and Myrtle, we were talking about you this morning, wondering how you're doing."

No mention of police searching for sweaters and other knitted things. Maybe that would come after they got through the greetings.

"I'm fine, thanks, Fannie. You?"

"Okay."

Still nothing about a search through everyone's wardrobe. That could mean Ike *had* sent the towel to the lab and called off the big search till the towel had been tested and no match found with the residue on the bottle. But she had to be certain.

"Fannie, the reason I'm calling—I think I left a barrette in the top, right hand dresser drawer. Could you check and see if it's there?" This would give her time to think of some questions.

"Sure, Beth. I'm in the kitchen so it won't take but a minute. Hold on."

She was back before Liz had time to think of something to say which would lead into talk about a police search—if there'd been one.

"I couldn't find your barrette, Beth. I looked in both top drawers to make sure. I'm sorry."

"That's okay Fannie. Thanks. I guess it's somewhere in my suitcase and I just didn't see it when I unpacked." She paused, thinking she'd have to come out with more of a direct question or she'd never find out if there'd been a search.

"How are things going over there?"

"Same as usual except everybody around here misses you, Beth. Miss Jane says it's not only because we haven't got a new maid yet. She says you were like a breath of fresh air in the house."

"Say hello to Miss Jane for me."

"I will."

"And Myrtle too."

"I'd put Myrtle on but she just went to her room for a nap."

This conversation was getting her nowhere, Liz thought. She'd give it one more try with questions more likely to evoke the kind of answer she wanted.

"Anything new? About the countess' death, I mean. Have the police come back to tell Mr. Alistair her death was an accident, after all?"

"Some cops came here this morning, but not to tell Mr. Alistair anything," Fannie replied. "They were in all the bedrooms looking for something, I don't know what."

Liz felt as if she'd been kicked in the stomach. There *had* been a big search. This sounded as if Ike didn't think Myrtle had anything to do with the murder and her towel wasn't important. After what he'd learned from the informant last night, he must have decided Miss Jane was the killer. He'd sent the towel to the lab to humor her, as if she were a child he had to pacify. She felt crushed, humiliated and betrayed.

A moment later an ugly possibility flashed into her mind, sending her spirits even lower. Maybe he hadn't sent the towel to the lab at all.

"Fannie, did you happen to notice what the police took?" she asked.

"Yes. I was upstairs doing the bedrooms when they came. They took things from everybody's drawers and closets. Mr. Randolph, he was complaining to his mother because they took a sweater he wanted to wear today. Then when the cops were leaving one of them told me they'd taken two scarfs and a shawl from my room and Myrtle's. Everything would be returned in a few days, he said."

Wouldn't Fannie know if the police had been in the laundry room and taken a towel?

Despite the rising lump in her throat, Liz managed to continue the conversation.

"I hope they found what they were looking for and they

won't bother you anymore. It's been good talking to you, Fannie."

"It was good to hear from you. Myrtle will be sorry she missed talking to Ducky. I'll be sure to give her your best when she wakes up."

In spite of her mental turmoil, Liz noticed Fannie's voice hadn't taken on its usual sharp edge, when mentioning Myrtle. "Are you and Myrtle getting along better?" she asked.

"Yes. You know how I couldn't stand her bragging about cooking dinner for the Prince of Wales and the rest of them. Well, she's stopped that. She's turned very quiet the last couple of days. Miss Jane noticed it too."

Myrtle quiet? Myrtle not bragging about her royal kitchens? She must be worried about her sister, Liz thought. "Well, I must go now, Fannie," she said, "so I'll say good-bye."

"Good-bye, Beth."

She'd always considered herself too strong and independent to shed any tears over a man, but now she felt the sting of moisture rising into her eyes. She took a tissue out of her purse, wondering if Ike had felt as bad as this when he realized she'd deceived him.

Did this mean he hadn't totally forgiven her? Was this his way of getting back at her?

She knew she had to pull herself together. Talking to Sophie would help. She dried her eyes and punched Sophie's cell phone number.

"Is this an okay time?" she asked, when Sophie answered.

"Yeah, but it wouldn't be if you'd called a few minutes ago. We just collared a punk who ripped off a deli and we're taking him to the house for booking. What's up?"

"I need to talk to you."

"What's wrong? You sound lower than a snake's belly."

"I guess I am. Can you meet me after work today?"

Sophie hesitated for a moment before replying. "Sure. Where shall we meet?"

Liz noticed the hesitation. "If you have plans . . ."

"Ralph and I were going to take in an early movie, but I'll cancel. What do you say you and I have dinner somewhere nice? How about our favorite Rock Center place?"

"I don't want you to break a date with Ralph just to have me cry on your shoulder."

"What are best friends for? So, are we on?"

"What would I do without you, Sophie? All right. I'll meet you there around six."

Meeting Sophie for dinner meant she wouldn't be home when Ike got to her place. She didn't want to see him, anyway. She should call him now and tell him she'd made other plans for the evening, but she didn't want to talk to him—not right now. Then she remembered he said he'd phone her office and let her know when he could make it to her place. She'd tell him then not to come over. There'd be no need for her to explain. His conscience would tell him why she didn't want to see him.

Speculation about Miss Jane and Myrtle had filled her mind from last night till only a few minutes ago. Now there was nothing left of the anticipation with which she'd wakened this morning. All she could feel was a deep sense of disappointment.

Chapter Seventeen

Sophie peered at Liz over the restaurant menu. "Do you want to tell me right now what's got you so down or wait till after we've ordered?"

"Let's order first," Liz replied. "That way we won't be interrupted."

"Okay." Sophie took a final glance at the menu. "I'm going to have the special. Have you decided what you're hungry for?"

Liz gave a sigh. "I'm not hungry at all, but I know I have to eat something—guess I'll have the special too."

"I've never seen you like this," Sophie said. "Not even when Lenny Kreutzer asked Michelle Vizzi to the Junior Prom instead of you."

Sophie could always make her smile. "Back then I suppose being dumped for Michelle Vizzi was just as bad as what I'm going through now."

A waiter appeared. They ordered. Sophie looked at her expectantly. "Okay, I'm all ears."

Liz began by telling her about the Scotland Yard check on Myrtle, then went on to her idea that the bottle might have been wrapped in Myrtle's towel. "If it was, it could have picked up lint and other residue from the bottle," she said.

164

"I get it," Sophie said. "You told Ike about it and he didn't think there was anything to your idea. If that's what has you down in the dumps, I'm surprised at you. I never thought you were neurotic."

"You won't think I'm neurotic when you hear the rest of it," Liz replied. She told Sophie everything.

Drawing the hurtful thoughts from her mind and expressing them out loud made her feel worse than ever. "Oh, Sophie, I thought Ike had come around to enjoy trading ideas with me. I never thought he'd treat me like a child just because he disagreed with my viewpoint."

"That doesn't sound like Ike. He wouldn't humor you like that. He'd tell you right up front if he thought your idea stunk. Seems like all you have to go on is your phone conversation with the maid."

"Fannie was very definite about what was taken. She didn't mention a towel."

"But you don't know for sure."

"Well . . . no."

"I take it you haven't talked with Ike since you got this crazy idea that he's humoring you and not being straight."

"No, we haven't talked since he told me on the phone that the towel was on its way to the lab. He was supposed to phone me at work to let me know when he'd be coming over to my apartment tonight. I was going to tell him not to come over, but when I left the office he hadn't called yet."

"He'll probably try to reach you at your place. When you don't answer, he'll try your new cell phone. Do you have it with you?"

"Yes, but I forgot to give him my number. I don't want to talk to him, anyway."

"You should at least let him know what's bothering you and give him a chance to explain."

At that moment the waiter arrived with their dinners. Sophie took a taste of hers before looking at Liz with a frown.

"I think you've blown this out of proportion. Why would Ike pull something like this?"

"To get even with me for lying to him about spending Memorial Day weekend with Gram."

"Oh come on—you know Ike wouldn't be so childish. You're the one who's being childish."

Liz sighed and shook her head. "I know I'm acting like an adolescent, but this has made me feel like I don't know him at all, and maybe I never did."

Sophie cast her a stern look. "Cut the dramatics. You sound like a character in a soap opera."

Depressed as she felt, Liz had to laugh. She and Sophie had been sharing their trials and tribulations since they were in grade school. They'd never failed to cheer one another up.

"Thanks, I deserved that," she said. "But what shall I do about this?"

"First, ask yourself how much of it is your imagination."

Liz pushed her food around on her plate while pondering the advice. "Maybe I did read more into it than was actually there."

"Most likely there wasn't anything there at all. I know Ike's in love with you, Liz. A man doesn't play games like that with the woman he loves."

Liz gave a wry smile. "If he's in love with me he sure isn't in any hurry to tell me he is."

"He still hasn't said anything?"

"A couple of times I thought he was going to, but then something always interrupted—like a phone ringing."

Suddenly Liz realized they'd gone to an entirely different topic. She grinned at Sophie. "You're good at this, you know."

"Does that mean you're feeling better?"

"Much better."

"Good. Why don't you give Ike a call right now? Tell him you'll be home in an hour. When he called your office and realized you'd left, he probably tried to reach you at home."

Liz hesitated. Her dwindling doubts had brought on guilt feelings. She wasn't ready to hear Ike's voice. "It's too late for him to still be in the squad room," she said.

"So try his cell phone. You know you have to talk to him sooner or later."

Liz wasn't certain how she'd react when she heard Ike's voice. Would her guilt for mistrusting him push her to the brink of tears? "I'm not ready to talk to him yet," she said.

"Meanwhile, the poor guy's been trying to get you at home and starting to wonder where the hell you are."

Liz still had enough hurt in her to make a defensive reply. "Well, it's not my fault he didn't call me while I was still at work."

"Come off it, Liz—you know when a homicide detective's on a case it takes priority over everything else. And with this new angle on Myrtle . . ."

"He doesn't believe anything's going to come of that."

"Maybe not, but he has to follow every lead. And speaking of leads—anything new on Miss Jane?"

"Oh, I've been so upset I forgot to tell you Ike had a meeting with an informant last night—someone who might know something about the murder of Miss Jane's husband."

"A jailhouse snitch?"

"Possibly. What if his information involves Miss Jane in her husband's shooting?"

"That would suggest she's capable of murder!"

Liz nodded. "The other day in the coffee house you mentioned blackmail. I've thought for some time that the countess might be holding something over Miss Jane's head."

"As far as we know, she's the only one the countess might have been blackmailing," Sophie said. "Nobody else had such a strong motive. Assuming Myrtle's towel is being tested, this murder seems like a toss up between Myrtle and Miss Jane."

"But what if nothing comes of the towel test and what if Ike's meeting with the informant is a dead end?" Liz asked.

"You can bet Ike and Lou haven't ruled out any of the others. Maybe Randolph's the guilty one, after all."

Liz felt her mind stirring as if a fresh gust of wind were blowing through, sweeping away the last shred of her despondency. "All of a sudden I'm dying to know what Ike's going to tell me. I'll call him on his cell phone now, and tell him I'll be home in an hour."

"Good," Sophie said.

Liz put in the call. Ike didn't pick up.

"Now *I'm* wondering where *he* is," Liz said.

Sophie looked at her with a grin. "Sounds like you've snapped out of your blue funk."

"You made me see what I knew in my heart all along. Ike would never do anything like this to me."

"Let's finish eating so you can get home."

There were two messages from Ike on her answering machine. "Sorry I couldn't call you at work—I was tied up," the first one said. "I'll give you time to get home and call again."

In the second message he sounded as if he were in a hurry. "Not home yet? Well, I wanted to let you know I can't make it to your place anytime soon—maybe not tonight at all. I'll try and call you later."

No mention of the test on the towel, but something important must have happened. She turned on the TV. Maybe whatever it was would be on the news.

She surfed through all the news channels, but none had any new developments in the Zanardi case. She switched to a movie channel. An old film was in progress. Watching Cary Grant and Ingrid Bergman would fill the time while she waited for Ike to phone.

The movie ended. It was 8:30 and still no call from Ike. She thought of his meeting with the informant. Something big must have come out of that. Something implicating Miss Jane.

What if the informant told Ike that Miss Jane killed her husband? Suddenly all previous possibilities became probable. The countess *knew* and was using this to keep Miss Jane in virtual bondage. The pieces of the puzzle were fitting together now, and the picture was starting to look like Miss Jane.

She switched to a news channel, thinking a bulletin might have come on while she was watching the movie. Evidently it hadn't. She checked the other news channels. Nothing about Miss Jane yet. Nothing on the Zanardi case but rehashes.

She decided to watch another movie. Checking the program schedule, she found an oldie with Fred Astaire and Ginger Rogers. That would do, she thought. Light entertainment she wouldn't get too drawn into. When Ike phoned she could switch it off without wondering how it ended.

It was 10 o'clock by the time Fred and Ginger executed their final twirls, uninterrupted by the phone. Nothing on the 10 o'clock news about a break in the Zanardi case.

She recalled what Ike had said in his last message on the answering machine. He wouldn't be over anytime soon and maybe not at all, and he'd *try* to phone her. To make sure, she replayed the message.

She knew he wouldn't drop in at this hour without calling first. She might as well get ready for bed.

She crawled into her sofa bed and reached to turn out the light when the phone rang. She grabbed it before the second ring.

"Ike?"

"Yeah. Sorry I couldn't call earlier."

"Where are you?"

"At the Hunterdon house. I have news for you."

Excitement sent her pulse racing. *News*. This must mean his meeting with the informant had paid off. That's why he was at the Hunterdon house. He'd gotten enough evidence to arrest Miss Jane for the murder of her husband *and* Harriet Hunterdon Zanardi!

A pang of sadness pierced her excitement. Deep sympathy welled in her heart for this good woman, driven to murder by cruelty and blackmail.

"It's over, isn't it?" she asked. "And it was Miss Jane, wasn't it?"

His answer left her in startled disbelief. "Yes, it's over, but no, it wasn't Miss Jane."

Chapter Eighteen

Not Miss Jane? For a few moments she was too surprised to reply.

Then, the incidents involving Randolph flashed across her mind. He claimed he hadn't heard the smoke alarm go off, although it was just outside his bedroom. He'd brushed past her in a hurry, coming out of the countess' bedroom. He'd been in the kitchen, walking towards her from the direction of the storeroom.

Could the killer be Randolph, after all?

Ike's next words surprised her all over again. "We just arrested Myrtle," he replied. "The towel test gave us everything we needed."

Again she was speechless. She'd made herself miserable by thinking he was humoring her, maybe even lying to her, about Myrtle's towel. She thought he didn't consider Myrtle a suspect. She'd been sure information from the snitch had led Miss Jane to confess she'd killed her husband *and* the countess. And then, when Ike said the killer wasn't Miss Jane, she could only think of Randolph.

"This can't be much of a surprise," he said. "You must have suspected Myrtle when you tipped me off about the towel."

Yes, she'd had her suspicions about Myrtle, but they'd

been lost in her foolish imaginings. "I wasn't sure you took the towel tip seriously," she said.

"During the past few weeks I've learned not to make light of any ideas you come up with," he replied. He paused. "Is it too late for me to come over to your place? I have a lot to tell you—not only about Myrtle, but Miss Jane too."

She'd lie awake all night if she didn't get the details about Myrtle and hear what the informant told him about Miss Jane. She knew she had to stretch the truth a bit.

"I'm still up. Come on over."

Depending on traffic conditions, it wouldn't take long for him to drive from the Hunterdon house to her apartment. She had to move fast. She got out of her pajamas and into shirt and slacks. She rushed to the bathroom to comb her hair and dash on some makeup. She'd just folded up the sofa bed when his knock came at her door.

In the midst of his hug and kiss she asked herself how she could have had even the slightest thought that he'd be anything but honest with her. A shrink might say it was because she wasn't sure about his feelings for her. Whatever the reason, she didn't need a shrink to tell her no matter how he felt about her she'd never doubt his integrity again.

Watching him sit down on the sofa, lean back and stretch out his long legs, she felt sure this was the first relaxation he'd had all day. He'd been going full blast since morning. He probably hadn't taken the time to eat anything other than a few bites on the run. But even if he wasn't hungry, she knew he'd always go for a cup of coffee.

"I'll make coffee," she said. "And how about something to eat?"

"Thanks. Coffee will go great. I'll pass on the chow. Lou and I grabbed some fast food before we went to the Hunterdons."

Her personal feelings and her concern for him had temporarily taken over her thoughts. Now questions about

Myrtle and Miss Jane crowded her mind. But she wanted to hear about Myrtle first. She started the coffeemaker and returned to the sofa, ready to tell him she couldn't wait another minute for his report.

He must have sensed her feelings. Before she could say anything, he laughed. "Okay, here goes. First, I might as well tell you while I was looking for the towel in the laundry room the search went on for the other articles."

"Didn't you believe there'd be a match with the towel?"

"I was pretty sure, but just in case that didn't happen, we decided it would save time if everything went to the lab and the towel tested first. Then if the towel tested negative, the other articles could be tested without having to go back to the Hunterdon house."

Hearing him explain made her feel guilty all over again for having doubted him.

"We didn't get the results of the towel test till tonight," he continued. "But around noon today I heard from Scotland Yard. They'd been digging deeper into that old case I told you about where Myrtle was questioned. It turns out there are startling similarities between that case and this one. The victim was female and the cause of death was smoke inhalation."

"Wow," Liz said.

"That's not even half of it," Ike went on. "Like the countess, the victim had been drinking heavily the night she died. Then she had a bedtime nightcap and passed out. There was a fire. Only in this case she actually had been smoking in bed. According to the report, there were cigarette butts in an ashtray on her nightstand. Her death was declared accidental, caused by the victim falling asleep and dropping a lit cigarette on the rug."

"But you said Scotland Yard first considered it homicide."

"Right. A charred cigarette was found on the rug near the bed. It had ignited a heavy, tapestry bed skirt and caused a smoldering fire. From the position of the cigarette on the rug, Scotland Yard believed, at first, that it couldn't have been dropped by the victim but was deliberately planted."

"It's eerie how much like the Zanardi case that is," Liz said. "Was the victim slipped something to knock her out before the fire was set?"

"The glass on the victim's nightstand was tested. Nothing showed up. Scotland Yard originally figured either the glass had been thoroughly washed or substituted. No prints on it."

"Didn't the autopsy show anything toxic?"

"There was no autopsy."

"No autopsy? Why?"

"The family didn't want it."

Alistair Hunterdon's objection to an autopsy on his sister was another similarity, Liz thought. "Why was homicide changed to accidental death?" she asked.

"The family of the deceased was one of Britain's most elite—wealthy, influential and politically powerful. For whatever reason, pressure was put on Scotland Yard."

Liz nodded. Pop had told her about cases in the United States where wealthy, powerful families used their influence to protect one of their own. "Was a member of this British family under suspicion?" she asked.

"Yes, the victim's husband—one of the family sons. The investigators found out they'd been having marital troubles. The old story—another woman in the picture. They also found out the wife refused to consider a divorce." Ike glanced over his shoulder. "Smells like coffee's ready."

"Coming right up," Liz said, heading for the kitchenette. She filled a mug for him and poured a glass of cranberry juice for herself. Coffee at this hour would keep her wired till tomorrow afternoon.

She returned to the sofa saying, "Why was Myrtle questioned?"

"All the servants were questioned. Myrtle was never under suspicion. In fact, she continued to work in the household for nearly two more years. That's why when I got my first information from Scotland Yard I didn't consider Myrtle a suspect in the Zanardi case."

"Did she work for that family till she came over here?"

"No. She didn't come over till more than a year after she left their employ. Yesterday, my contact at Scotland Yard interviewed members of that British family and found out Myrtle left them of her own accord. She took a leave of absence saying she needed to rest. They expected her to return but she never did. They lost track of her after a while. Apparently they weren't aware she had a mental illness."

She looked at him, startled. "How did you find that out?"

"My Scotland Yard contact did some digging."

"How serious was it?"

"Serious enough for her to spend several months in a psychiatric care facility after she left the household. My contact at Scotland Yard located a doctor who'd treated her, but all he could find out was that Myrtle had been put on medication and released."

"If Scotland Yard was right at first, when they said the British woman's death was a homicide, do you think Myrtle did it?"

Ike shook his head. "But when we questioned her about it, she told us she and the other servants didn't believe it was an accident. She said they all thought it was murder. That put us onto the idea that the Zanardi murder was a copycat crime."

"Myrtle thought the British husband had gotten away with murdering his wife, so she used the case as a pattern."

"Exactly. She admitted it. And she also admitted she didn't realize there'd be a mandatory autopsy on the countess. She said that worried her for a couple of days, but when nothing was reported about a toxic substance in the countess' system, she thought it hadn't been picked up. She believed she'd gotten away with it."

It was Myrtle who'd planted the seed of doubt about the

cause of the countess' death, and got everyone believing it was accidental, Liz thought. It was part of her copycat crime.

"Didn't the British family notice anything strange about Myrtle?" she asked.

"Only that she had an exaggerated opinion of her cooking skills and constantly made grandiose claims to anyone who'd listen that she was the best cook in England. She claimed that the cooks at Buckingham Palace were using her recipes."

Liz thought of something Pop told her. In his long experience as a NYPD homicide detective he'd run into more than a few killers with severe mental problems. She recalled him telling her about a case where a killer made grandiose statements about his family background. He had what Pop described as a narcissistic personality. Pop told her such mental cases suffer mood swings not unlike bipolar disorder. They can get so caught up in their grandiose self-images that they can become capable of committing crimes to get what they believe they're entitled to.

She related this to Ike. "Do you think Myrtle could have a narcissistic personality?"

"I don't have your pop's lengthy experience with the homicidal mentally ill," Ike replied. "But it sure sounds like it. Thanks for the helpful input." He paused. "Myrtle was on medication. She didn't say, but maybe she stopped taking it and that's what set her off."

Liz nodded. "She told me she cut down her doses a few weeks ago. She thought the medication was increasing her appetite."

"More helpful information. Without adequate medication, Myrtle's dislike of the countess went out of control." He paused. "Myrtle was clever. I can't understand why she didn't get the bottle out of the house. I know live-in servants stay put except on their time off, but Myrtle must have had a couple of days off since the murder when she could have gotten rid of the bottle."

"She never got the chance," Liz replied. "She didn't get her usual day off during the week following the countess' death. Fannie told me Miss Jane wanted both of them to stay in till after the funeral. And then . . ." She recounted her experience with Myrtle on Sunday morning.

"She seemed troubled and uneasy. I thought she was worried about her sister who's in a nursing home with Alzheimer's. Now I realize she was planning to get the bottle out of the storeroom and was waiting for me to leave the kitchen so she could go in there and get it, unnoticed."

"Would it have been unusual for Myrtle to go into the storeroom?" Ike asked.

"Yes. The whole time I was there I never once saw her go into the storeroom. Even Fannie, who'd worked there for years and knew exactly where to find things, didn't go in there often. If Myrtle had gone in there on her day off, when she was all ready to leave, I would have been curious—maybe even suspicious, and I guess she knew it."

"If you hadn't been in the kitchen, she'd have taken the bottle away and we'd have no evidence," Ike said. "You're an incredible woman, Liz Rooney. You know I disapproved of you being undercover in a house with a killer on the loose, but now I'm beginning to look at it in a different light."

"I was never in any real danger," Liz replied. "And please don't remind me about Randolph."

"Okay, but I'll remind you that Myrtle could have turned on you like she turned on the countess."

"Myrtle was no threat to me. She told me she'd taken a shine to me. She called me Ducky."

"You could have been a dead Ducky," Ike growled.

Liz laughed as she shook her head. "Myrtle considered the countess phony nobility, and because this bogus countess showed no respect for someone who'd cooked for real royalty, she grew to hate her. In her badly skewed reasoning she probably believed that getting rid of such a person was justifiable."

"No shrink could have said it better," Ike said. "If by some miracle Myrtle is judged fit to stand trial, you'd make a great witness for the defense."

"Sounds like you think she'll be declared unfit."

"Yeah, I do. She's had this condition for years and it's gone from bad to worse."

"Doesn't the Bureau of Immigration have regulations about letting people in with diagnosed mental illness?"

"I think it depends on the individual case. Myrtle's illness was being controlled by medication. Also, she needed to come here to care for her ailing sister. That might have worked in her favor."

"When you got the second report from Scotland Yard telling you about Myrtle's mental illness, I guess you took it straight to the DA?"

"Yeah. He agreed if the lint and hair and bits of gluey paper on the bottle matched with what was on Myrtle's towel, we'd move on her."

"How did Myrtle react when she was arrested?"

"She didn't show much of a reaction. She was very quiet. When we read her her rights she said she understood, and she didn't need a lawyer present, and she wanted to make a full statement."

"Was she taken to jail, or what?"

"She's being held in a psychiatric facility. Her condition will be evaluated before any court proceedings take place."

"Can you give me a rundown on what she said and how she carried out her murder plan?"

"In her statement she said she was angry with the countess for making her do work she considered beneath her. She knew about the vodka bottle in the nightstand. She'd noticed it and a pack of cigarettes and matches in there while she was straightening up the bedroom. That Sunday she was cleaning the countess' bathroom, growing angrier by the minute she said, when she got thinking about the death of the woman in the London home where she worked."

With a grin, he lapsed into an imitation of Myrtle's East End accent. "Died breathing smoke from a fire in her bedroom, she did. All us servants suspected the husband done the lady in. But when the police said the fire was set with a cigarette on the carpet and called it murder, the family said it was an accident and put up such a scrap that the police gave in."

"Nice takeoff," Liz said, laughing. "That's why Myrtle decided she could copy the crime and get away with it."

She pictured Myrtle pouring detergent into the countess' vodka bottle to make sure she'd pass out before the cigarette was planted. She imagined her waiting till everyone in the house had gone to bed and she felt sure the countess had swilled down the detergent, then getting a bottle of vodka from the household liquor supply and sneaking up to the countess' bedroom.

"I know you got the picture," Ike said.

Liz nodded. In her mind's eye she saw Myrtle switching the bottles, planting the burning cigarette and returning to her room with the other bottle. She'd wrapped it in the towel and hid it in her room, intending to rewrap it in newspaper and get it out of the house on her day off during the week.

"During the police search, she must have concealed the bottle under her apron, still planning to get rid of it on her day off," Liz said. "When her day off was cancelled, she must have gotten nervous about keeping it in her room, so she wrapped it in newspaper, sneaked into the storeroom at night and hid it there. She intended to get it out of the house on her day off, Sunday. She hadn't counted on me being in the kitchen Sunday morning. She thought I'd be upstairs doing the bedrooms."

"I think you figured it out, exactly. She had a very clever plan."

"Pop told me people with mental disorders of this type are generally very clever," Liz replied. "But Myrtle wasn't quite clever enough."

He flashed a grin. "Not with a certain Irish redhead on the case. Which reminds me, I have a question I never got around to asking you. What made you decide to search the storeroom?"

"If I tell you, will you promise to go easy on me?"

He gave a puzzled smile. "Sure."

She told him how her wildfire imagination led her from suspecting Randolph to searching the storeroom. She'd never live this one down, she thought.

She finished with a sigh. "Well, now you know how I happened to think of looking in the storeroom. You can tease me about my overactive imagination now if you want to, but not too much, please."

"No teasing this time," he said. "If it hadn't been for your imagination you'd never have found the bottle."

"That's true. And speaking of the bottle, how did everyone in the Hunterdon house take it when you told them Myrtle put household cleaner in the countess' vodka?"

"They were stunned about that and about Myrtle's mental illness too. But when the shock wore off they took it very well. Alistair Hunterdon apologized for having doubted the accuracy of the autopsy. They all seemed sorry for Myrtle. Fannie and Miss Jane said they'd noticed her mood swings."

Liz recalled Myrtle's kindness towards her and the devotion shown the sister in the nursing home. "I can't help feeling sad," she said. "Myrtle showed me a different side."

"Be thankful you didn't get mixed up with the other side. I know you believe she wouldn't have harmed you in any way, and maybe you're right, but whenever I think of you in that house, I thank God it turned out the way it did. If anything had happened to you . . . if Myrtle had . . ."

She'd never seen him so wrought up. "Don't you know I'd have been out of there like a shot if—"

"Liz," he interrupted, taking her hand, "there's something I've been meaning to tell you. I shouldn't have waited this long to tell you, but better late than never, right?"

She stared at him. What was he going to tell her? Could it be what she'd been hoping for? What else could it be?

"Right," she replied.

"After all the clues you came up with and the homicides you helped me solve, there's a close bond between us," he said. "So I guess you have a pretty good idea what I'm going to say."

Her heart went into a spin. "Please, just tell me," she whispered.

Chapter Nineteen

He tightened his hand with hers. "I want to tell you how much I value your input into my cases," he said.

She felt as if she'd been pushed into a pool of icy water.

"This case, especially," he continued. "If you hadn't found the bottle and come up with your idea about the towel, I don't know how we'd ever have figured it out."

She hoped her disappointment didn't show in her eyes. Somehow, she thought of a response to replace the one half-formed in her mind. "You know I enjoy matching wits with you."

He gave her a hug, saying, "I guess now you'd like to hear about my meeting with the informant, and what I found out about Miss Jane."

She summoned a smile. "Of course I would."

"Okay, here goes. A couple of years ago this informant was doing time for armed robbery when he struck up a friendship with a guy in for assault and battery. To cut the story, the assault and battery con came down with a terminal illness and landed in the prison infirmary . . ."

Some of Liz's disappointment receded. Her thoughts raced ahead of his words. She pictured a deathbed confidence to a prison friend. And it had something to do with

Miss Jane. "Did this sick con tell the other one who killed Miss Jane's husband?" she asked.

"Right. He said *he* did it, but he didn't know the identity of either the husband or Miss Jane. He was a thug for hire."

A hired killer! Liz saw it all come together. Miss Jane had been living in constant fear of a drunken, abusive, bum of a husband who squandered her earnings on booze and threatened to track her down and kill her if she left him. She'd taken what she believed was the only way out.

She shook her head. "Poor Miss Jane. She must have been driven to desperation—hiring a hit man to kill her husband."

"This gorilla didn't kill," Ike said. "He just made people *wish* they'd been killed. But something went wrong that time. Miss Jane's husband wound up shot dead in an alley outside a bar and the gunman was never caught."

"You said he didn't know Miss Jane's identity or her husband's. Then your informant wouldn't know their identities, either. How did you put all this together?"

"The dying con told his friend he wanted to get something off his chest before he died. He said nine years ago he made a deal with a woman, a total stranger to him, to rough up her husband so he'd never be able to abuse her again."

"That woman was Miss Jane," Liz said.

"Right."

"But how would someone like Miss Jane contact a hit man?"

"He didn't say who put her on to him. Someone in one of the joints her husband frequented, maybe."

"She might have gone there looking for her husband and got talking to someone."

"That's probably how it happened. Anyway, this thug told his friend he always kept a gun on him but he'd never had to use it. But while the hit man was carrying out the contract, the woman's husband pulled a knife on him."

"The hit man shot him in self defense," Liz said. She sighed. Nice, gentle Miss Jane contracting with a thug to disable her husband for the rest of his life! But at least she hadn't intended to have him killed. No wonder she was in such bad shape when the countess took her in. She must have been overcome with remorse.

"The dying con told his friend he'd never killed anyone before," Ike continued. "He wasn't a religious man, he said, but he had to tell someone before he died."

"Well what do you know—a thug with a conscience," Liz said. "So how did his friend happen to contact you?"

"Like I said, my informant didn't know the name of the victim or the woman who made the deal, but when he got out of jail he phoned our squad room to discuss peddling information about a nine-year-old cold case. I happened to be the detective he talked to. He said think it over and he'd get back to me about a deal."

Liz nodded. The ex-con expected to be paid for his information. Pop had told her about prison informants.

"From what he said on the phone, I thought this case had similarities to the unsolved murder of Miss Jane's husband. When I met with the snitch, it turned out I was right. I paid him for the information out of my own pocket, incidentally."

"Why? I thought the department took care of compensating snitches."

"That's true, but when he gave me the full details, I was sure Miss Jane was that anonymous woman and this could make her a prime suspect in the Zanardi case. I decided to keep it to myself for a while. I didn't even tell Lou."

Liz knew this wasn't the first time Ike had shown compassion for a suspect. In many ways he was like Pop, she thought. He could be as tough as any hardboiled TV cop character, but he had a tender place in his heart.

"When the informant first contacted you, how did you hook Miss Jane up with what he said?"

"While I was interviewing members of the Hunterdon

household, Fannie the maid told me all about Miss Jane.
When the ex-con mentioned a nine-year-old cold case on
the phone, I saw the parallels."

"Was that why you came back to the house that day—
to try and get Miss Jane to talk about her husband's shooting?"

"That was my intent. I thought if I could get her to admit
being involved in it, the rest would all come out. She'd tell
me the countess knew about it or found out about it and
was holding this over her head."

"And then she'd confess she'd killed the countess and
the case would be solved."

"Yeah. I asked her a few questions about the countess,
but I never got around to grilling her about her husband's
death. Call it instinct or a hunch, or whatever. I decided to
give it a little more time. Meanwhile we'd concentrate on
the other suspects."

"Was she your prime suspect all along?"

He gave a rueful smile. "I have to admit she was high
on the list till a certain savvy redhead set me straight." He
reached over and drew her into his arms. "It's getting so I
can't solve a case without you."

She thought of making a flip remark—something like,
"Yeah, right", but the look in his eyes suggested this wasn't
the appropriate time for it. A moment later she *knew* it
wasn't. They were locked in a kiss that made her forget
everything else.

When the kiss ended she thought this would be the perfect moment for him to tell her what she thought he was
going to say, before. But the moment passed in silence.
They might as well have just gone on talking about Miss
Jane.

With the thought of Miss Jane, a question landed in her
mind. How was Ike going to handle the case of a woman
who'd hired someone to disable her husband?

"I have something to ask you about Miss Jane," she said.
She knew it wasn't what you usually said when you'd just

come out of a wonderful kiss and you were still in a guy's arms and he showed no signs of letting go.

If he considered the remark ill timed, he didn't show it. Ike wasn't one to let his reactions spread all over his face. But she felt his arms relax, slightly. "What do you want to know?" he asked.

"What's going to happen to her?"

"If you're asking if I'm going to reopen that nine-year-old cold case, the answer is no."

I should have known, she thought, smiling into his eyes. Only the two of them knew Miss Jane's secret. What would it accomplish to let it out? After too many hellish years with a brutish husband and another nine with her supposed friend and benefactor, she deserved her peace. Miss Jane believed her secret had gone to the grave with Harriet Hunterdon Zanardi, and Ike was going to keep it that way.

She kissed him—a kiss as tender as the place in his heart. "It's no wonder I'm crazy about you, Detective Eichle."

This time his emotions showed in his eyes. "You must know how I feel about you, Liz. I've been trying to get the right words together . . ."

Sophie said with Ralph she had to give it a shove . . .

"There's nothing complicated about getting three little words together," she said. "Look. Read my lips—"

He interrupted. "I can't. When I look at your lips the last thing I want to do is read them."

Before she could think of an appropriate reply, he tightened his arms around her. "But I got the message anyway," he said. "I love you too, Liz Rooney."